NIGHT ON THE WATER

The Mason Braithwaite Paranormal
Mystery Series, book 12

In this series:

Signs Point to Yes

The Desert Rats

Reach for the Sky

Billy Blood

Rubber-Band Ball

The Invisible Arrow

Penstock Canyon

The Man from Grapalia

The Mythical Blond

Stealth Glasses

The Melted Pineapple

Night on the Water

The Landers Mystique

NIGHT ON THE WATER

NIGHT
ON THE
WATER

CHRISTOPHER CHURCH

DAGMAR MIURA
LOS ANGELES

Published by Dagmar Miura
Los Angeles
www.dagmarmiura.com

Night on the Water

First published 2020

ISBN: 978-1-951130-31-2

ONE

THE NORTHEAST WASN'T THE best place to vacation in winter, but Mason tagged along with his boyfriend, Ned, when he went to a conference in upstate New York. Mason had spent a couple of days on his own exploring the town, even though it was hard to see it under all the snow, until he lost feeling in his toes, which usually took an hour or so. At that point he'd retreat to a coffeehouse to warm up. But that was all done with, and they were on the way home, changing planes at O'Hare in Chicago.

The plane stopped at the gate, and the chime sounded, and people started to get up and pull down their suitcases and heavy winter jackets. Ned stepped into the aisle and stretched, revealing the pleasing musculature of his torso under his shirt, and Mason got up, glad to be on his feet even though he had to stoop under the bins. Airplanes were built for petite people, not anyone like Mason, over six feet tall and with a rugby build. With Ned in the aisle, he took half a step closer and was able to stand erect. He ran a hand through his thick red hair. What a relief.

They were near the back, and even up front by the door there was no sign of movement, the aisle now full of bodies and wheeled suitcases. A guy wearing a tweed jacket and carrying a violin case pushed past Ned from behind.

"Excuse me, please," he said. "I have a connecting flight. It's boarding right now." His accent was detectable but slight, maybe Slavic, and he was in his forties, with gray streaks in his dark hair.

"Good luck with that," Ned said, shifting to let him get by as he pushed ahead.

The man turned back to Ned long enough to flash a smile and say, "Oh, thank you, sir."

Ned leaned toward Mason and spoke quietly. "He was being sincere."

"He didn't understand what you meant," Mason said. "It's the language gap."

"I feel like a total dick now," Ned said, and

they watched the man push past another person, then climb over a suitcase.

"There's nowhere to go," a woman said to him, raising her voice as he tried to squeeze by. "You're going to have to wait with the rest of us."

"We're probably going to miss our connection too," Mason said.

Ned nodded. "We've definitely missed it. There's no point in rushing."

Eventually the horde started to shuffle up the aisle, and they made it out into the terminal. Mason arched his back and twisted his shoulders to make sure nothing had permanently seized up in the confined position. The gate for their connecting flight wasn't far away, and when they walked up, they could see the aircraft outside, slowly backing away from the ramp into the darkness. Standing at the little counter talking to the agent was the man with the violin case. Mason and Ned lined up behind him.

"That's the guy who shoved past me on our flight," Ned said.

"It is. This is totally going in my coincidence journal."

Ned eyed him. "I thought there were no coincidences."

Mason had to smile. He'd often said that. Ned was just throwing it back at him. Ned didn't believe in psychic power, and thought Mason was deluded in his career choice, although he had come to respect the fact that Mason could make a living with it.

"If they don't exist, why do you write them down?"

"Because lots of them are synchronicities," Mason said.

"How is that different?"

"A synchronicity is a meaningful coincidence. Something I need to pay attention to."

At the counter, the agent was finishing up with the violinist, and pulled a narrow card from her printer.

"You'll get to LA tonight, just a little late," she said, and handed him the boarding pass.

The guy thanked her and turned away, studying the document, then looked up, and catching Ned's eye, smiled broadly at him before he walked off.

"You have a new friend," Mason said.

"It's because I have such good manners, and treat everyone with unwavering respect."

Mason chuckled at that, then stood aside when the agent waved them forward. Ned could handle the rebooking for both of them.

When Ned stepped away from the counter, he waved the new boarding passes and said, "We got seats on a later flight. There's about ninety minutes to kill."

"Right on. Let's get something to eat."

Walking around the terminal, they eventually found a burger joint that had a meatless option, so they sat at a table and ordered. While they were waiting for the food, Mason pulled his coincidence journal out of his backpack. It was a pocket-size red-bound notebook, and he opened it to a blank page and jotted down the date, then wrote:

> On the first flight, a second-language guy with a violin case thanked Ned, not recognizing his sarcasm. The guy was also on our connecting flight.

Synchronicities were a psychic tool that helped him tease out connections that might provide him with insight, illustrating disparate parts of reality that were linked in invisible ways. Not all coincidences were meaningful, but it didn't hurt to keep track. He glanced up to see Ned, watching him write, the slightest trace of a smile on his lips. He was so handsome, with dark Latin features, his hair nattily coiffed and perfectly tousled, his shirt immaculate even after hours in that cramped airplane. It was impossible to resent him for his skepticism, as he mostly kept it to himself.

The waitress came by with two glasses of water for them, then turned to the next table. In front of a guy in a well-worn brown suit, she set down a highball glass with an inch of amber liquid in it.

"What kind of burger stand serves hard liquor?" Mason said quietly.

"These people do things differently. We're just not familiar with their ways."

"Chicago's not exactly the backwoods of Siberia or the Congo Basin."

Ned shrugged. "It's what happens when you leave Cali. All logic, all reason, all sense of order just break down."

Mason folded up his journal and snapped on its elastic closure. "I'd say you're looking forward to getting home."

••••••••

WHEN THEY LINED UP to board the next flight, Mason saw the guy with the violin case ahead of them, walking down the ramp to the airplane amid the stream of other passengers. As they boarded he saw him put his case into the overhead bin, then take a seat against the window. Ned glanced at his boarding pass and stopped in the aisle right where the guy was sitting, then heaved his bag into the bin. When Mason checked his seat number, sure enough, they were in the same row. Mason stepped in to take the middle seat, beside the violinist, leaving the aisle for Ned.

"I hope you have your coincidence journal handy," Ned said, dropping into his seat.

"The red-headed man," the violinist said, his tone jovial, watching him dig for the seatbelt.

"I'm one of them, at least," Mason said, settling back.

"You also came from Ithaca."

"I guess we missed the same connection."

"Do you live there?"

"In Los Angeles."

"Me too—I'm headed home. I'm Rovski."

"Mason," he said. "This is Ned."

Ned nodded hello, then looked back to his phone, clearly not willing to engage.

"Were you in Ithaca for the university?" Rovski said.

"For a real estate conference. Ned is in that business."

"I was at the university. I teach math."

"Interesting," Mason said, and averted his gaze, settling into his seat and looking to the window as the plane lurched back from the gate.

"So what's your work?" Rovski said.

"I do research."

"In science?"

"I'm an investigator."

"You mean like a private detective?"

"Similar, but I'm not licensed," Mason said. "I don't carry a gun."

"I'm glad to hear that, seeing as we're sitting on an airplane." He shifted in his seat, leaning closer. "Maybe you could do some research for me. Do you have a business card?"

Stretching his leg and reaching into his pants pocket, Mason found one, smoothing out the dog-eared corner before he handed it over.

"Mason Braithwaite," Rovski said, reading from the card. "That's an unusual family name. What's the ethnicity?"

"I thought it was English, but English people say it's not. To them it's a Danish colonial name from a thousand years ago."

Rovski scoffed. "That's why I left Europe. They're stuck in the past—limited by it. A thousand years and you're still a newcomer. California is just the opposite. It doesn't matter so much what your pedigree is or how long you've been there. The focus is on the future."

"I've never lived in Europe, so I can't compare."

"Do you think all the developments in technology could have come from Zagreb, or London, or even New York?" He waved his hand for emphasis. "Never. Look at your cell phone. Such innovation is only possible in California."

"Isn't the tech industry more about the Bay Area?"

"It started there, sure, but it's bleeding south. And the culture is the same."

"I don't see that," Mason said. "People are way more uptight up there. But the idea of innovation fits. Los Angeles has always been about getting a fresh start."

"Reinvention," Rovski said. "That is the great opportunity of our city."

"I guess the downside is that all that tech-industry money makes it expensive for the rest of us."

"Why does it say 'psychic investigator'?" he asked, looking at Mason's business card again.

"I'm a psychic. I use psychic insights to gather information that's not apparent to the regular senses."

"But psychic power isn't real."

Mason sighed and looked out the window again, watching the blue ground lights roll by as the plane taxied. "A lot of people think that way."

"Maybe the important word is *research*. You can do regular detective work, can't you? That's what I need."

"If you want to come to my office, I can look at your case and decide whether or not I could help you."

"You're in the Primavera Building. That's downtown?"

"Correct."

"Shall I call your office to make an appointment? I drive through downtown on my way to work."

"I don't have staff," Mason said. "That number

is for me directly."

"Will you be in the office tomorrow?"

"I can be."

"So I'll come in the morning."

"Let's make it after lunch," Mason said, eyeing him.

"I'll be there." Rovski tucked the card into his breast pocket.

The engines were revving up as the plane made a final turn and paused, preparing to take off.

"I'm going to put my earbuds in, for the noise," Mason said, and sat back, closing his eyes.

Once they were aloft, he drifted off, lulled by the sound, and found himself riding an airboat, whipping through the saw grass, the engine and the giant fan roaring behind him. Reaching out, spreading his palm, he could feel the fine spray of water kicked up by the power of the boat.

●●●●●●●

THE RUMBLE OF THE tires meeting the runway woke him, and Mason shifted up in his seat.

"LAX, baby," Ned said, and squeezed his hand.

Rovski was reading something on a tablet—it was in the Latin alphabet but the words weren't in English. He must have felt Mason's gaze, and looked up at him.

"I'm definitely looking forward to getting out of this tin can," Mason said.

"Actually, it's mostly made of carbon fiber and titanium. Also aluminum."

He chuckled. "It's just an expression."

"Well, it's an inaccurate one."

When the plane stopped moving and the chime went off, Ned was quick to his feet, pulling their bags down and handing one to Mason. Once it was their turn to walk out, Mason said good-bye to their seatmate.

"See you tomorrow," Rovski said pointedly.

Once they'd walked through the terminal and stepped out onto the curb, Ned looked reenergized, pointing the way to the right bus stop.

"*Hola*, civilization," he said.

Mason glanced at the roadway, the multiple lanes of cars and buses crawling past, honking at each other, the noxious smell of diesel in the air.

"I wouldn't call this civilized," he said. "Everyone hates this airport."

"Love it or hate it, it's ours."

"At least there's no snow. I guess there's something civilized about being able to feel my toes."

The shuttle came eventually, nosing through the snarl of noisy traffic. Sitting together on the bus, Ned put his arm around Mason's shoulder.

"I can't wait to get that shirt off you and get you into bed."

Mason looked at him sidelong. "I can't believe you have that kind of energy right now."

"I don't," Ned said. "Not really. It's just bluster. I'm exhausted—I can't wait to get my own shirt off and crash out."

The shuttle dropped them at the hotel garage where Ned had parked, and they climbed a flight of stairs and walked the row of cars until they came to the familiar Crown Vic. It was a classic sedan that Ned kept in pristine condition with the help of his gearhead brothers. They climbed in, and Ned started the engine, studying the instrument panel.

"Still half a tank, just the way I left it."

"You thought someone might take it for a joy ride?" Mason said, pulling on his seatbelt.

"People siphon gas out of vehicles in these long-term lots. It's been a problem for years."

"That seems so desperate. Gas isn't that expensive."

"The more income inequality there is, the more theft," Ned said, turning to look out the rear window as he backed into the aisle.

"And you call that civilization."

"It's not utopia, but I do love it."

"I guess I do too." That was the other side of it, Mason thought. The extremes of wealth and poverty were the counterpoint to Rovski's idealized future-oriented paradise.

Once they were on the freeway, Ned merged into the carpool lane and gunned it. The trip home to their hilly neighborhood north of downtown went quickly, the roadways uncrowded so late at night.

Driving up the narrow hillside road to their house, Ned said, "Matt's here."

Mason saw what he was talking about as they pulled into the driveway and waited for the garage door to roll up: Matt's SUV was parked on the street out front, right behind Peggy's little Prius. Their roommate, Peggy, had been dating Matt for a while, and he slept over sometimes. Four people were a lot in a small house, but Matt was a friend of theirs too, and he was pretty easy to get along with. Most importantly, he didn't hog up the bathroom in the morning.

The lights were off and Peggy's bedroom door was closed when they got in. Mason dropped his bag on the chair in the corner of their bedroom, then went back to the kitchen to guzzle a glass of water. Ned was already naked and climbing into bed when he got back, and in moments they were both asleep.

TWO

WAKING WHEN HIS BODY wanted to, not troubled by an alarm, Mason got up and pulled on a pair of sweatpants and a T-shirt. Peggy and Matt were both gone, and Ned was working in his office, halfway down the hall to the living room. Mason poked his head in the doorway.

"Have you had breakfast?"

"Hours ago," Ned said flatly.

Mason went out to the kitchen and fired up the espresso maker, pouring almond milk on a bowl of muesli while he waited for the machine to heat up, then dumped the whole pot of steaming black happiness into a mug. Sitting on one of the barstools at the counter between the kitchen and the living room, he imbibed as much of the coffee as he could, then munched on some fruit and the muesli and looked at his phone. It was going to be overcast all day, apparently, but it wasn't supposed to rain.

After a second pot of espresso, when he was starting to wake up enough to face the traffic, he got dressed. He'd wear a jacket, he decided. Unlike Ithaca, there was no snow, but it was still winter. Once he'd pulled it on and slung his backpack over it, he wrapped a Velcro strap around his pant leg to keep it out of his bicycle chain, then stopped in Ned's office to kiss him good-bye.

Mason's bicycle was allowed a small patch of real estate in the garage, well away from Ned's two babies, the Crown Vic and the even older Barracuda. He was lucky to have it, he knew, as Peggy had to park on the street. Wheeling his bike out of the garage, he cycled down the hill, deftly rounding the curves and picking up speed, the cold air in his face exhilarating. Through the bougainvillea hedges at the foot of the street, he turned onto the boulevard and rode to the metro station, where he carried his wheels down the stairs into the earth.

The downside of taking his bike on the train was that he had to stand with it the whole way, but it wasn't that far to get downtown, and soon he was climbing up out of the ground again, admiring the pink terra-cotta of the glamourous Primavera Building. Dating to the art deco era, it always raised his spirits to come here and walk inside.

In the lobby, the security guard was sitting at a desk near the door.

"Annette," he said, greeting her as he went by.

"Hey, Mason," she said, looking up briefly and glancing at his bicycle.

He didn't bother to tell her that he had a visitor coming later, as they didn't stop people coming in during business hours. With his foot he kicked down the bicycle stand, parking it in the lobby for as long as it took to duck into the mail room, manipulate his keys to open his box, and pull out the bundle of paper.

Back by the elevators, he pressed the call button and wheeled his bike to the doors where the vintage sign above lit up to say THIS CAR UP. Upstairs he paused to wrangle his keys again, admiring the raised yellow lettering that stood out sharply on the black surface of his office door:

MASON BRAITHWAITE
PSYCHIC INVESTIGATIONS

His suite was one big room, with exposed brick and concrete floors, austere and modern compared to the restored mahogany and decorative flourishes of the lobby. There was a wide patch of open floor near the door where he parked his bicycle, and at the back were a restroom and a storage space, where he kept his espresso maker. In the middle of the room was a round table and chairs for meetings and séances, and under the tall windows that looked out on the Financial District was a set of lounge furniture with his cobalt-blue sofa.

He dropped his mail on his desk, which was positioned to face the windows. All the furniture had come from the thrift store, and none of it was as tony as the surroundings, but his clients never commented on that, instead focusing on the view.

The best thing about the building was the white light streaming in the glass door from the stairs in the corner. Suspended in the middle of the stairwell, a glass column transmitted visible light and less tangible positive energy down from the roof, a feature that the building's architect had incorporated in the original construction. It made him feel like he was meant to be here, doing his metaphysical job next to that metaphysical channel. The place suited him, and he wasn't even paying rent—he'd made an under-the-table deal with the landlords to help them out on a real estate deal, and in return they had agreed to let him use the office rent-free.

Mason had just pulled his computer out of his backpack and set it on the desk when there was a sharp rap at the door. Rovski was early, he thought, and strode over to pull it open. Standing there he found not Rovski but Hanh. Petite and with a sharp wedge haircut, Hanh was a colleague in the psychic field, ostensibly running a nail salon on Sunset Boulevard in Hollywood. But Mason knew she had a lot more going on, and had a significant role in the unseen world—as an overseer, maybe, or something like a bouncer. He'd witnessed some of her supernatural abilities, far beyond any psychic skills that Mason could muster. She'd saved his butt once, and later she'd tasked him to work with her.

She smiled at him. "You look good."

"Back at you," he said, even though he couldn't see in her any difference from any previous encounter. "Come in."

Mason closed the door as Hanh stepped over to the windows.

"I love this building," she said. "It's such a gem."

"Do you want something to drink? I can make espresso, or I might have a bottle of water."

"No thanks."

She sat on the cobalt sofa under the window, and Mason joined her on the adjacent wing chair.

"I can't stay long," she said. "I wanted to talk

about your current client."

"I'm not actually working with anyone right now."

"You will be, then. The violinist."

"Rovski. I met him last night. He said he'd come in today." Mason didn't bother to ask how she knew about him—over the course of their relationship he'd learned that she was indifferent to the flow of time, experiencing the past and the future at will.

"I'd like you to work with him," she said.

"That's the plan, if I can help him. Do you know what he wants me to do?"

"No idea. But you should work with his dream self."

"You mean using lucid dreaming? I use dreams sometimes to get insight."

"Not like that," Hanh said, and frowned. "I mean you have to connect with him in the dream world as well as in this world."

"I thought my dreams were just for me."

"You meet people in your dreams just like in waking life, don't you?"

"Sure, but it's not really connected to real life," Mason said. "It's like an echo of my daily experiences. A hazy mirror."

"You're wrong to dismiss it as a creation of your own mind," she said, holding his gaze. "The people you encounter there are as real as you are, and that place is as real as this one."

Mason thought about that. "It doesn't seem like it. When I wake up, it's kind of malleable and unclear, and it quickly fades."

"That's a translation issue. Your brain struggles to retain information from a system that works on different assumptions. Next time you're there, think about this place—your office, this city. It'll seem just as disconnected and unreal."

"So how will I find Rovski when I'm dreaming?"

"You said you know how to lucid dream. That's all you need."

It felt counterintuitive, but Mason couldn't disbelieve it, not after everything he'd experienced with her. Hanh knew more about the intricate folds of reality than he ever would.

"What kind of tools can I use?" he asked.

"Lots of that world bleeds through into waking life, although it's not always evident. Look for familiar things."

"What do you mean?"

She gestured helplessly, then waved a hand at the illuminated glass door to the back stairwell. "Like a doorway. It isn't just a doorway. It means the beginning of something, or a change of conditions, new parameters."

"That's so vague."

"Also remember that time and space work

differently. They're less important than here." She rose and smiled. "It's good to see you."

"That's it?" Mason demanded. "I have no idea what you're asking me to do."

"Just what I said—connect with the violinist's dream self, in addition to the version of him here."

"'Version'?"

"When you're talking about a multidimensional personality, the dream version and the version you've met are a little different."

"So Rovski is a multidimensional personality?"

"Everyone is," Hanh said, and frowned. "You know that."

"I guess I should know that. Maybe I do, intuitively."

"You'll figure it out," she said, and strode toward the hall.

Mason closed the door behind her and stood at the windows. He folded his arms and gazed absently out at the office towers and the streets below. Things were never really clear with Hanh. She just expected him to know. Admittedly he usually learned something when he was working for her, and he inevitably sharpened his psychic skills. But the ambiguity was annoying, and it was a lot of work. He needed to steel himself for that now—hard work in unfamiliar territory.

A knock at the door interrupted his thoughts,

and he pulled it open to find Rovski, wearing the same tweed jacket he'd had on last night on the airplane. He broke into a big smile.

"Hey, Red—look at you."

"Don't call me that," Mason said flatly.

"You look tired," Rovski said, unfazed, and stepped inside.

"I guess I'm still worn out from the trip. Flying is so dehydrating."

Pausing to look out the window, he put his hands on his hips. "This is such a beautiful office."

"It has a great view. Do you want an espresso?"

Rovski turned to meet his gaze and spoke ardently. "Oh, I love you, Mason—yes, please."

Walking over to his espresso machine, Mason had to grin. It wasn't every day he heard those words, although they might carry less weight in other languages. What Rovski meant, at least, was evident. He pressed ground coffee into the filter and attached it to the machine, then switched it on and watched the steaming hot java stream into the little pot. Once it was full, he poured it into two demitasse cups and carried them over to the lounge furniture, setting them on the coffee table.

Rovski sat on the sofa where Hanh had been just minutes ago, and Mason grabbed a notepad and a pen from his desk before he joined him.

"So delicious," Rovski said, cradling the cup and sipping from it.

Once he'd settled into the adjacent chair, Mason wrote "Rovski" at the top of the page, and drew a line under it, then looked up.

"So what can I help you with?"

"I think my coworker is trying to steal from me. We share an office."

"Back up," Mason said. "Where do you work?"

Rovski frowned. "I thought I told you on the airplane. I'm an associate professor of mathematics at Rayborn College. I share my office with another professor. Her name is Emily Luton-Jones."

"What is she stealing from you?" Mason said, as he scrawled down the woman's name, and the name of the college.

He shrugged. "You tell me."

Mason's eyes narrowed as he assessed his visitor. Very bright people sometimes thought about the world in incoherent ways. Rovski was hard to parse, and Mason couldn't tell yet whether he was one of those or just a guy with a screw loose.

"What happened with Emily?"

"I overheard her talking about obtaining funding. She used that word, *funding*."

"Is it for her research?"

Rovski waved impatiently. "Emily doesn't do research. She thought I wasn't within earshot. I heard her say that she would transfer thirty grand to *fay-thun*, and then she said, 'I'll make sure there's another fifty by next week.'"

"*Fay-thun,*" Mason said. "Is that a person's name, or a business?"

"Who can say?"

Mason sighed. "Can you spell it?"

"I can't do that. I've only heard it spoken. But I can write it phonetically." He waggled his fingers for the notepad.

Mason flipped over the top sheet and handed it to him, along with the pen. In a tight blocky hand, Rovski wrote a string of characters, then handed it back:

feɪθən

"Did you ever study languages?" Rovski said, leaning toward him.

"Not formally. Just taco-cart Spanish."

"Well, this is the sound of the word, even though I don't know what the word is."

"I recognize the upside-down *e*," Mason said, "but is this one a math symbol?"

"It's a Greek letter called theta. We use it in math too, but here it means the *th* sound. Not many languages have it. In English, it's the legacy of your northern European linguistic history— your family's ancient Danish roots. The Greeks use it too."

Rovski pointed to each letter, sounding them out individually. Absorbing it all, Mason drew an arrow to the theta and wrote, "Greek for *th* sound."

"So why does this mystery word mean that she's stealing from you?" Mason said, looking up.

"I don't know if she's stealing from me or not. I want you to find out. I also have more evidence in my office that I can show you. I haven't been to work yet since last night, or I would have brought it with me."

"What kind of evidence?"

"Paper," Rovski said, and gestured broadly. "Documents. Maybe she's not stealing. Maybe she's trying to frame me for something. Maybe she's embezzling money from the school, and it's a conspiracy with others." He raised his eyebrows. "To be honest, I'm afraid of her."

Mason watched him for a moment, and decided that rang true.

"What I'm hearing is that you think she's up to something, but you don't know what."

"I know it's something sinister. She used my login credentials on the school computer system."

Finally, something tangible, Mason thought. "How do you know she did that?"

"Whenever you log in, the page shows a line of text that says 'most recent login,' with the date and time. It's a security measure. Most people ignore it, but I'm a detail-oriented person."

"That makes sense." The guy was a mathematician, after all, and a musician, both skills that required attention to detail.

"I logged in and saw someone had been using my account just a few minutes earlier," Rovski went on. "It wasn't me, but Emily was in our office then."

"But you didn't catch her actually doing it."

"I know it was her. It can't be anyone else."

"How can you be sure?" Mason said.

Rovski shifted uncomfortably. "I keep my password on a piece of paper under the blotter on my desk. No one else except her uses my work space. She's the only one who could have seen it."

"Do your students come into your office?"

"Never without me being there, or Emily. And they'd never sit at my desk—but she does."

"Do you know what she did when she was using your account?"

"Who can say? But it can't be nothing."

"Did you change your password?"

Rovski frowned. "I can't. That would tell her that I know what she's doing."

"You have to change your password," Mason said emphatically. "You can make it look like a routine change. Write it down again under your blotter, but write it down wrong. Change a few of the letters. That way it won't look suspicious, but she won't be able to use your account again."

A smile spread across his face. "That's so smart. I knew you were the right man for this."

It was really just common sense, Mason

thought. That was another failing of brilliant thinkers—maneuvering through the mundane parts of everyday life sometimes stumped them.

"So can you look into her?"

"I'm not really that kind of investigator. I do psychic work."

"But you do real research too. I know you do, or you wouldn't have this fine office." He waved his arm at the room. "Unless you're looking into a crystal ball, and telling teenagers about their future love interests?"

"I don't do that," Mason said sharply. He actually had used a crystal ball in his work, but not the way Rovski was implying, not to scam people.

"Psychic power is just wishful thinking," Rovski said, folding his arms. "You're seeing patterns where there aren't any."

"So why are you here?" Mason demanded. "Psychic power is part of how I do my research."

"It was pure chance. An airline computer program put your seat next to mine. Just when I was thinking that I needed help to find out what Emily is doing to me, you sat beside me on the airplane and told me that you do research."

Mason closed his eyes and took a breath. Rational people could be so irrational sometimes.

"It sounds like you're the one seeing patterns where there aren't any," he said.

"You're a detective," Rovski said. "You can use psychic power on this if you want. I don't care, as long as you can do real things too. I just need help with Emily's skulduggery."

Mason wrote "skulduggery" on his notepad, and fleetingly wondered how Rovski had learned English, picking up words like that. The job would be welcome, as things had been slow. More importantly, Hanh wanted him to work with this guy, even though his ask was so woolly.

"Do you know anything about the dream world?" Mason said. "Like lucid dreaming?"

"I don't dream very often. I'm too tired from my work."

"Everyone dreams, and it happens every night. That's scientific fact."

"Then I don't remember my dreams," Rovski said. "What's lucid dreaming?"

"It's when you become aware inside the dream. You can take action rather than just following along."

"That's not something I've ever done," he said, furrowing his brow. "Why is it important?"

"It might not be." Not to his waking self, anyway. Mason wasn't about to tell him about Hanh's loopy ask, especially if the guy was skeptical of the metaphysical realm.

"I'm a rationalist," Rovski said. "Dreams and tarot cards and séances don't fit in my worldview.

But please don't think I'm judging you for your beliefs."

"It's more than belief—it's how I know the world works."

He nodded. "Math intersects irrational thinking a lot. Historically the boundary wasn't clearly defined."

"You just said you weren't judging me, and then you call me irrational."

"It's not your fault. People are hardwired to be superstitious. Like the number 108."

Mason clenched his teeth, suppressing his reaction. "What about the number 108?" he said evenly.

"It has some unusual properties, so in ancient India they theorized that 108 represented the entire universe. Even today in yoga they do 108 sun salutations, and there are 108 primary Vishnu temples."

"What are its unusual properties?"

"It has a lot of divisors. When you start playing around with it, it acts a little strange. The point is, it's an example where you can see math bleeding into an illogical system."

"I've never used math in my psychic work."

"What about counting the *I Ching* sticks, or astrology? Astrology is all about geometry."

"I know it's possible to use numbers to conjure meaning," Mason said. "My thinking is that it's like looking at clouds, or smoke, or tea leaves. It's just a medium to project something from your subconscious into the external world, so you can assess it with your conscious mind. Personally I'd rather do that without the math."

"I hope you can do that in my case."

"How about this: I'll come by your office, and you can show me the evidence you have."

"So you'll take the case," Rovski said, sitting forward. "Excellent. What is it going to cost me?"

"Five hundred a day."

His expression shifted. "I hope you can work fast. Does that include today?"

"Starting when I come to your office."

"Can you come tomorrow? There are a couple of time blocks when Emily will be teaching in a classroom but I won't." Rovski reached for the pad again, and jotted down a number. "That's my cell phone."

Mason pulled out his own phone and thumb-typed the number. Rovski had written a crossbar through the 7—the guy was definitely European. He sent him a text:

Mason cell

"Did you get that?"

Rovski pulled out his phone, and Mason heard it chime.

"Is this different from the number on your

business card?"

"It's the same one," Mason said. "Now you don't have to check the card." It also meant that the number Rovski had given him was legit.

Tucking his phone away, Rovski rose. "I'm glad you're willing to look, at least. I hope you can help me."

"I'll do my best." Mason followed him to the door and closed it behind him.

The guy was odd, but not crazy, he decided, and sat in the wing chair again to do a quick psychic assessment. Clearing his mind, he focused on the memory of Rovski, his eyes and his voice and his subtle accent. Were there any warning signs? Pushing away the random ordinary thoughts that popped up, he made room for true insight from outside his own mind.

The image that eventually coalesced was of twilight, a broad pink band along the horizon, the way it looked in the east just after the sun went down on the opposite side of the sky. The western sky probably looked like that at sunrise too, although he was never awake for those. Maybe that was significant—he should seek information on the other side of the sky, away from the main event. Opposite, far from the focal point, but still related.

Opening his eyes again, he got up and went to his desk, where he pulled open his laptop. A search for "phonetic spelling" led him into the system that linguists used to represent sounds. It was complex, with dozens of characters that indicated pronunciation and tone and stress.

Languages were not among Mason's strengths. Ned's *abuelo* sometimes tried to get him to speak Spanish, and he stumbled through conversations with him, thinking he was doing OK until the day he told Ned that they had discussed a trip the old guy had recently taken to Memphis. Ned didn't know about that trip, and eventually it turned out the guy had never been there, had never said anything about Memphis. Mason wasn't sure what he'd really heard, but he knew then that he needed to be less confident about his comprehension.

Digging through the phonetic alphabet, he found each of the symbols that Rovski had written down. The guy knew his stuff—they corresponded to the way he had pronounced the word he'd heard, *fay-thun*. Cutting and pasting the individual characters, he was able to recreate on the screen what Rovski had written in the phonetic alphabet. Next he pasted the string into a search engine. The first result that came up was an encyclopedia entry for "Phaethon (ˈfeɪθən)."

This was progress. He sat up in his chair and scrolled through the article. Not in contemporary use, it was a name from Greek mythology. Phaethon was a young man who was born to a mortal woman and fathered by the god Helios. Scanning the story, Mason decided to read Ovid's telling instead, and took a minute to pull that up. He had read a lot of Greek mythology since he'd worked the Mythical Blond case, and Ovid was his favorite source—he was such a good story-teller, and included all the florid details.

Phaethon was an irresponsible adventurer, it seemed, who borrowed his father's car, the vehicle that carried the sun across the sky each day. *Car* meant a horse-drawn vehicle, Mason realized. The meaning of that word had shifted in the hundred years since this translation had been written. Phaethon couldn't control the horses, and running wild, he set the landscape on fire—in Ovid's words, dark forests were ablaze, and rivers turned to steam. Even the Nile shrank and buried its source. Eventually Phaethon wound up dead as a result of his recklessness.

There was a moral message in it, Mason thought, sitting back in his chair. Something about the risk of overconfidence, maybe, and the inexperience of youth. However it tied in to Rovski's office mate, it was unlikely to be as lurid as this.

Shifting gears, he found that the college had a profile for Emily Luton-Jones, with a portrait of her, looking relaxed and smiling. In her forties, maybe, she wore simple jewelry, a gold necklace that looked warm against her dark skin. Her hair was done up in myriad elegant little braids. That would have taken a while. It was surprising how much women invested in their hair—the time, the money. Mason only got his own cut when Ned told him it was time.

Emily seemed down-to-earth, he decided, reading her brief biography, even though her name made her sound pretentious. He had half expected a Brit with a title and a family coat of arms, but this Emily had gone to a state college, and claimed heritage in Fresno, which was far from an ostentatious town.

His phone buzzed in his pants, and he pulled it out to check. It was a text from Ned:

Gilbert here for dinner. Peggy out for the evening. Baked okra.

It was close to the end of the day, and the overcast sky beyond the windows was shifting to darker gray. Packing up his computer, he pulled on his jacket and his backpack and wheeled his bicycle toward the elevators, pausing to lock the office door.

Okra didn't sound particularly mind-blowing, but whatever Ned was cooking would be good, he knew, standing beside his wheels and swaying with the motion of the train. Ned was a skilled vegan cook, and he and Peggy had bonded over it, collaborating and learning from each other over the last few years. Lucky for Mason, neither of them had tired of the hobby yet, which meant he ate well, and only had to help clean up once in a while.

Cycling up the hill to their house got him breathing hard, and he parked his bicycle in the garage before he went inside. Gilbert was already here, sitting on a stool at the kitchen counter. His dark Latin coloring was like Ned's, but everything else about him was a stark contrast—his wild tangle of hair, his unshaven jaw, the ill-fitting sweatshirt and ratty jeans.

Ned called, "Hey, babe," from the kitchen.

Gilbert stepped over to greet him, wrapping his arms around Mason's shoulders and planting a louche wet kiss on his neck. For a self-declared straight guy, Gilbert was awfully familiar.

"You're sweating," Gilbert said, pulling back.

Mason set down his backpack. "That hill isn't getting any less intense."

Gilbert guffawed. "Respect—I couldn't do that on a bike."

"I'm used to it, but I still sweat," Mason said, and stepped toward the kitchen. "Do you want a beer? I have some Kronenbourg in the fridge."

Holding his gaze, Gilbert spoke solemnly. "Are you sure that's what we want to do right now?"

"I don't really care whether you have one or

not. I'm just offering."

"Personally I would feel bad drinking around Ned when he's sober."

"Ned doesn't care," Mason said, frowning as he paused in the kitchen doorway.

"That's not your call," Gilbert said. "You need to take a look at yourself and your behavior. Smash that entitlement."

"What are you talking about?" Mason demanded. "I'm not entitled. I can barely make rent."

"It's not about what you have. It's about what's in your mind." Gilbert tapped his temple with his index finger.

Mason threw up his hands. "I've seen you drink around Ned."

"That's all in the past. I'm trying to expand my horizons, and get woke."

Mason turned to Ned, who was wearing his white apron over a dress shirt, both hands in a mixing bowl with a mass of green vegetables. "Am I an entitled ass for drinking around you?" he said. "Am I sabotaging your sobriety?"

"I didn't say you were an ass," Gilbert said, resuming his stool at the counter. "That's labeling."

"I'm glad there's a word for it," Mason said flatly.

"It doesn't bother me if people are drinking," Ned said. "You know that. Plus I'm dry, not sober.

My sobriety is a work in progress."

"So there you have it," Gilbert said, eyeing Mason. "You need to check yourself before you wreck yourself."

"Did the space brothers tell you that?" Mason said, raising his voice.

Gilbert frowned. "Don't act like you didn't see them yourself."

Mason sighed. He had to admit that he had, when he was working the Penstock Canyon case—a trio of gray aliens in Gilbert's bedroom. He didn't like to retrieve the memory, as it was too eerie, and he certainly didn't want to do anything that might attract them. But Gilbert's contact with those entities had become important in his life, giving him a sense of purpose, like the keel that kept him on tack. Right now, though, it felt like Gilbert was on an irrational tangent, and it was aimed squarely at Mason.

"I need to change," Mason said, and went down to the bedroom, pulling off his jacket and stretching out on the bed to cool off.

THREE

A WHILE LATER, NED SHOUTED to him, "Soup's on."

Mason sat with the pair of them at the dining table, and the food was delicious, as always. Ned had managed to cook the okra without it being slimy, instead making it tender and spicy and flavorful. A salad of romaine lettuce on the side provided the perfect crunch to complement it.

"I'm loving this dish," Mason said, savoring the okra.

"Me too," Gilbert said, and gestured with his fork. "So I met two women the other day who speak exactly three words of English."

Ned chuckled. "What was their first language?"

"Who knows? They looked European. If you draw a circle on the map between Berlin and Beirut, there are, like, eight hundred languages spoken in that area. It's probably one of those."

"Where did you meet them?" Ned said.

"They were trying to use the ticket machine at a metro station in Highland Park."

Mason frowned. "You were on the metro?"

"I saw them having trouble with the machine, so I pulled over to help them. It was one of those stations that's right beside the street."

"So you stopped your big honking SUV on a busy boulevard," Mason said, "and got out to help them buy metro passes?"

"It wasn't that busy. I put my flashers on."

"What were the three words?" Ned asked.

"*Oh, god,* and *no.* They kept saying it as I was helping them: 'oh, god, no.' They both had big puffy hair and short skirts and spike heels."

There it is, Mason thought. That's why he stopped.

"My first thought was 'human trafficking,'" Gilbert continued, "but thinking about it, there are no strip clubs anywhere around there, so I pulled over. They really were lost."

"Why were they saying 'oh, god, no'?" Ned asked.

"I'm not even sure they knew what that means. I told one of them, 'You need five dollars. Do you have any cash?' I showed her a ten-dollar bill, and she said, 'oh, god, no,' but then she pulled out a twenty. I asked them, 'What station are you going to?' The other one said, 'oh, god, no.'"

Ned laughed. "Were they high?"

"Not at all. They're just not from around here. I showed them the board with the route map, and they said, 'oh, god, no.'"

Listening to the story, Mason had to laugh. Gilbert really was entertaining. The guy was eccentric, he reminded himself, not malicious.

"Mason has a new European friend too," Ned said.

"He's a client, not a friend," Mason said. "Although he did tell me 'I love you' today."

"What the hell?" Ned demanded, with mock ire. "That rumpled little rat needs to keep his grubby paws off my man."

"It was a language thing. I offered him a coffee, and he was happy. A native speaker would have said something like 'I'd love that.'"

"Is he hot, at least?" Gilbert said.

Mason eyed Ned. "What's your assessment?"

"I'm sure to some people he is," Ned said. "Although you're not going to see him on the catwalks in Milan."

Forking up the last of the okra on his plate,

Mason explained how they'd met Rovski on the plane.

"So what does he want you to do?" Gilbert asked.

"I'm not sure yet. So far it sounds like office politics."

After they'd eaten and chatted for a while, Gilbert got up and moved toward the door, pulling on his jacket. Before he left, he put a hand on Mason's shoulder and kissed his cheek.

"You'll think about what we discussed?" he said.

"Sure," Mason said, and held his gaze for a moment, struggling not to scowl at him.

Gilbert hugged Ned good-bye and went out.

"That boy is a handful," Mason said, once Ned had closed the door.

"He's a great storyteller."

"Mostly because he gets himself into such crazy situations."

Mason helped him clean up, then followed him to bed, still wiped out from traveling and changing time zones. Once he was under the covers, Ned picked up his tablet, and Mason lay close to him for a minute, relishing the warmth of his skin. Eventually he rolled to his own side, thinking about his day, the odd visit from Hanh, and the perplexing Rovski.

There was still work to be done tonight, if

he was going to track down Rovski in his sleep. Although he knew the theory behind lucid dreaming, he'd never had much luck with it, and rarely got more than vague hints about his cases. Hanh had talked about symbols—keep an eye out for them. Sleep soon loomed, and he sank into the hypnagogic state, his mind a jumble of images and colors and sounds.

He was walking up a street that had a bit of an incline, not as steep as the hill to his house, but still a noticeable grade. There weren't any cars around, just the dark pavement, brick buildings looming close to the sidewalk, and shadows cast by the moonlight. It was wider than his street too. *This is a dream.* He needed to become aware. The realization started him in that direction, and he gradually came to awareness, focusing his thoughts, struggling his way into lucidity. It looked like Ithaca here, although there was no snow, and he could still feel his toes. *Rovski,* he remembered. He needed to find Rovski. But how was he going to do that? He was a stranger here, and didn't really speak the language, like those women Gilbert had met at the metro station.

Then he was there, standing at the ticket machines at the station in Highland Park. Funny how dreams work—disconnected, jumbled. *Time and space work differently,* Hanh had said. Of course they did. That was self-evident. He didn't need to have it explained.

Lucid, he told himself. Stay lucid. There were people on the platform, waiting for the train, but he looked away. He didn't need to be here. Rovski—he thought about the guy's face, his goofy smile and graying hair, the contours of his accent when he spoke. Then he was back on the hilly street again, only this time he could hear music. Fiddle music, he realized, fast and peppy. Rovski played the violin, and the violin was interchangeable with the fiddle.

Walking toward the sound, he crested the hill and found the guy who was playing. He wore red suspenders over a dark shirt and trousers, an old-fashioned worker's cap on his head. This had to be Rovski. Younger, and thinner, and with a different face, but it was him, he just knew it. As he played, he met Mason's eye and grinned. His identity was there, unmistakably, in his gaze— those were Rovski's eyes.

When he looked down, Mason saw there was a violin case open at his feet, with some shiny coins in it and a few crumpled singles, along with a small orange. That was an odd thing to leave for a busker. The color was so dark and rich. It was probably a tangerine. The fruit expanded in his awareness as he remembered the scent, the tartness, the texture. But it wasn't important now, and it wasn't why he was here. He pulled his attention away from it. Digging in his pocket, he found a few coins and tossed them into the case.

The guy stopped playing. "Hey, thanks," he said.

"For the music."

"I figured."

It was curious that this guy didn't have any trace of Rovski's accent. "Where did the tangerine come from?" Mason asked.

"That's a good question. Where did you come from, stranger?"

"I'm not a stranger. I'm Mason."

He cocked his head. "That doesn't sound quite right."

"Dude—I know my own name."

"If you say so," he said affably, and waved his bow.

"What's your name?"

"Herman."

As he said it, Mason could feel the weight of it. It was important, he knew that. He could use it to find the guy again later. But how did he know that? It was an insight, he decided, not just a guess.

"Herman," Mason said, repeating it again so that he'd remember.

"That's me."

"Have we met before?" Mason asked. "On the way from Ithaca, in Chicago?"

"Ah, Ithaca," Herman said, and gestured broadly with his bow. "Home of Odysseus. They called him the cunning king. He was a sailor, like you."

"I'm not a sailor," Mason said, and frowned. "And you're talking about the Greek original. I meant the one in upstate New York."

"If he was cunning," Herman said, "why did it take him ten years to sail across the Aegean and around the butt end of Greece? That doesn't seem all that smart to me."

"Maybe cunning isn't the same as smart. You have to admit he did pretty well, considering what he came up against."

"Lots and lots of inclement weather," Herman said flatly. "If you believe his version of it. But I do love that tale."

"Why are we talking about Odysseus? It's a different Ithaca."

"Right—the one in upstate New York. Now, Chicago, there's a whole other story. That's where they serve bourbon in burger joints."

Mason watched him for a moment. "You pulled that out of my memory. It means you're just something I generated in my own head." He clicked his tongue. "I was so sure you were real."

Herman scowled. "I'm as real as you are, Stretch."

"Sadly, I know that's not true. I made you

up because I wanted to find you. It's just wishful thinking. Why else would you bring up the bourbon at the burger joint?"

"You know as well as I do there are background connections among people and events. Just because you can't see them doesn't mean they don't exist." He waved the bow and added emphatically, "I'm not from inside your mind."

He was right, Mason knew, that things were connected in ways that weren't always obvious, or linear, or rational. He should know better than to make a snap judgment.

"Tell me something that couldn't be from inside my own head," he said.

"You're testing me now?" Herman demanded. "Coming at me like Achilles?"

"Humor me. I'm a stranger here."

"Fine," Herman said flatly, and looked away, furrowing his brow in thought. After a moment he straightened up and held his instrument behind his back. "Answer me this: how many strings are there on a violin?"

"I have no idea," Mason said, thinking about it. "Six? Eight? Maybe eight is too many. Six. Or maybe it's five."

"Let's go with this—you don't know," Herman said. "Sometimes they have six, but a standard violin is like mine." He held it out for Mason to see.

"Four strings," Mason said, looking closer. "Who knew?"

"You certainly didn't. When you get home, look it up. It's objectively true, and it didn't come from your own mind—it came from mine."

"That would convince me. I'll remember to check." Eyeing him, Herman still had a scowl on his face, so Mason added, "I hope I'm not being a dick here."

"Denying my existence definitely falls into that category," he said, but then his expression softened. "I know you're new at this. You'll get the hang of it."

With that, Mason lost his lucidity, and sank deeper into the void, beyond the reach of memory.

FOUR

THE HOUSE WAS QUIET when he woke up. Peggy always left early on weekdays for the school where she taught, and when he grabbed his phone from the bedside table, he saw that Ned had left early too:

At a meeting on the Westside today.

Rovski had texted him as well, giving him the window of time when he'd be in his office and Emily would be in classes. It wasn't until early afternoon, but it meant he had to get out of bed now. Bracing himself for the cold air, he pushed off the covers and got up.

After he pulled on a pair of sweatpants and a shirt, he went out to the kitchen. Beyond the French doors in the living room, the balcony was wet, the railing and the outdoor furniture still dripping. It wasn't raining now, but the heavy clouds remained, drifting toward the east. Once he had a pot of espresso made, he sat at the kitchen counter and pulled open his computer. He'd heard of Rayborn College but didn't know exactly where it was.

In Rio Bosque, he saw, gazing at the map. Was that a red flag? Mason had worked undercover at Rio Bosque city hall, investigating a crooked politician. Repeated interviews with sheriff's deputies in uncomfortable little rooms, and hours of sitting for depositions with testy lawyers—he didn't have fond memories of the place. Sliding off the stool, he went to retrieve his coincidence journal from his backpack, and jotted down the details:

> Busted the mayor of Rio Bosque. Rovski's college is in Rio Bosque.

It wasn't ominous, he decided, rereading the page. It might not even be meaningful. Just to be sure, he closed his eyes and cleared his mind, waiting for any sign that he was wrong.

Herman, he remembered. Herman said violins had four strings. The details of the encounter flooded back into his mind. It hadn't faded like dreams usually do, but he'd forgotten about it until now.

Looking at his phone, he checked, and it was true, four strings was the standard. Four little strings, so close together. It didn't seem like a lot of real estate to generate the wide gamut of noise that came out of a violin. In any case, it meant that Herman wasn't imaginary, and Mason's initial insight was valid. Herman was connected to Rovski—a version of him, to use Hanh's word. The disconnect was that Rovski was so obtuse, and Herman seemed functional and self-aware. But trying to stay lucid in an unconscious state was new to Mason, so maybe he didn't have the means yet to interpret that world.

Once he'd eaten some muesli and an orange, he checked the weather. It wasn't going to rain again, so he didn't bother putting a jacket on over his sweater. Rayborn College was too far to cycle all the way, and he spent a minute with the map, figuring out the best place to get off the metro. He'd have to change trains, and then cycle the last few miles.

••••••••

An hour later he was rolling up on the sprawling campus, just starting to dry out from the overnight storms. It had the unmistakable vibe of an educational institution, with broad lawns and walkways, and a hodgepodge of buildings in styles spanning the decades. Throngs of students filled the paths, and Mason stopped for a moment, straddling his bicycle, to ask one of them where building 12 was. Following the directions he was given, he found its entrance, with a long bike rack just outside. But he stayed on the path and cycled past it, gawking to get a sense at the building.

On this side the structure had big windows looking out over the lawn. It was hard to date the architecture, but it definitely wasn't new. The far side had a pedestrian entrance similar to the one next to the bike rack, and once he'd circled around the back, he found a paved driveway and a couple of loading docks. Pedaling back to the entrance with the rack, he locked up his wheels among the myriad others, then made his way inside.

Walking into the wide hallway was like time-traveling, with the classic lighting fixtures, wood paneling, and ornate decoration that fortunately hadn't been updated during less stylistically enlightened times. It wasn't as old as his office building, more likely dating to just after the war. A row of cubicles made of dark-stained wood still bore the inscription TELEPHONE above each booth, although the equipment inside was long gone. They had no doors, just a little bench, but each of the spaces would be a comfortable place to make a cell phone call. A woman was inside the last one, putting it to just that use, leaning on the bench and talking into her phone, gesturing animatedly with her free hand. Even though he'd never used a pay phone, the booths evoked warm nostalgia for another era, putting a smile on his face.

This floor seemed to be classrooms, with big double doors. Catching a glimpse of one of the spaces as a stream of students made their way inside, he saw a whiteboard and a lectern facing a sea of desks.

Rovski's office had to be below this level, based on the room numbers here. Finding a flight of stairs, he trotted down and strolled the hall until he eventually found the right number. The signs mounted beside the doorway read z. ROVSKI and E. LUTON-JONES. Mason had assumed that Rovski was his first name; what did the Z stand for?

Mason rapped on the door, and a moment later Rovski pulled it open, beaming at him. The office was long and shallow, with a row of narrow windows just below the ceiling. It had felt like he'd come downstairs from the ground floor, but this must be a semi-basement, as it still had natural light. The desks were built into a long counter, one at either side of the room, with a printer between them and cabinets underneath. Along the wall opposite each desk was a trio of armless straight-backed chairs. That's where a visiting student would sit, and not linger, as they didn't look very comfortable.

"You found me," Rovski said.

"It's a great campus." Mason set his backpack on one of the chairs. "Are your classes in this building?"

"Mostly, and also in some other places." He dropped into his desk chair and gestured to the row of guest chairs. "Have a seat. I'm sorry I can't offer you a lovely espresso, like at your office."

There were some similarities between Herman and Rovski, he decided, watching the guy as he spoke. Especially around the eyes. As Mason sat down, the hard slats against his back confirmed that these chairs weren't built for lounging.

"Did you ever read the *Odyssey*?" he asked.

Rovski's eyes narrowed. "Are you saying this investigation will be lengthy and rife with delays?"

"No," he said flatly. "I'm talking about the actual epic."

"I know it's a convoluted story, and a very thick book. I never sat down with it. But it's baked into Western culture from the foundations—I'm sure I've read many parts of it over the years, or at least heard the stories. It's the tale of the Trojan War?"

"It's about Odysseus and what happens to him after the war. It takes him ten years to get home."

"That seems excessive, even for a time before airplanes. Why are you asking me about it?"

"Just curious," he said, and waved a hand. Clearly Rovski didn't share Herman's interest in the Ithacan king.

Rovski swiveled around to his desk and pulled open the bottom drawer, producing a single sheet of paper.

"Evidence," he said, handing it to Mason.

It was a statement for a bank account, specifically one of those tax-exempt retirement savings accounts that employers sometimes paid into. Mason turned it over to glance briefly at the back, covered with dense gray microprint, presumably containing every disclaimer the bank's lawyers had ever written. He looked over the details on the legible side. The account had nearly four million dollars in it.

"This has your name on it," Mason said.

"Correct. I found this in the scanner." He gestured to one of the machines on the counter between the desks. "It means she digitized it but forgot to take the original. She's secretly acquiring my details."

"What use would this be to her?"

Rovski shrugged. "I thought you might know."

"Where did she get your bank statement?"

"It was in my desk drawer. It's not always locked. I used to think I didn't need to impose high security in my own office."

"Are you sure you didn't leave it in the scanner yourself?"

"Of course I'm sure." He scowled. "Look through the paper in the light."

Mason held the sheet up to the window, and instantly saw it—a small patch was darker, less translucent than the rest of the page. Looking closer, he saw that the dark bit contained part of a number, in the box that showed the account balance. A little rectangle of paper with numbers on it had been stuck on top.

"It's been altered," Mason said.

"I didn't do that. Why would I do that? She did it, and I want to know why."

"What was the original balance?"

"Around twenty-three thousand dollars. The four digits with the comma, 3,921, were glued over the 23. The numbers are the same style, so she must have cut them out of a similar document. Maybe another statement from the same bank."

"You and Emily are the only ones who use the scanner?"

"It's wired into our computers. No one else can access it."

Mason looked over the page again. "So Emily added almost four million bucks to your savings."

"How could it benefit her?"

"Did you confront her about this?"

He shook his head. "I know she would only deny it. She would smile and say she knows nothing about it. Then she would become more secretive. I want to find out what she's plotting without her knowing what I know."

"Do you have any financial entanglements with her?"

"You mean like business deals? There's nothing like that."

"She's not the beneficiary of your will, or your life insurance?"

"Of course not," Rovski said.

"Is there any reason she might think she is?"

"We share this office, and go to some of the same meetings. We've never even had a meal together. Do you think she's trying to steal my money?"

"I can't see how forging this would help her do that. If the four million isn't really in the bank, no one can get it, regardless of what this piece of paper says."

"That's what I thought too. So she must be trying to frame me for something. Maybe she wants to tell the college that I'm a thief."

"I don't think that's what's going on. You could easily clear up any questions with an unaltered printout of this document."

Holding the page up to the light again, he

studied the outline of the superimposed paper. Why would someone do this? He could feel himself getting drawn into the mystery.

"I definitely want to look into it," he said finally. "What else has she done that's suspicious?"

Rovski's brow furrowed in thought. "Using my computer account, like I said. I also saw her going into one of the technology buildings on campus on two different days. It's not forbidden or anything, but people in the math faculty would have no reason to go in there."

"Maybe she has a friend who works in that building."

"That's possible, but it's full of scientific equipment, so it has security. You can't take any food inside because there are clean rooms. It's difficult even to get through the door. People who work in that place have to leave even to get coffee."

"So she's not going in there to socialize."

"It's not that kind of place. They call it the Bunker. The windows are covered with a mesh to block radio waves."

"They don't want radio waves going in, or getting out?"

"Both. It's to protect the experiments. Cell phones don't work in there, and there's no Wi-Fi. I often see people standing around outside the entrance checking their messages."

"Which building is that?" Mason asked.

"Building 42. I'll show you."

Turning to his computer, he pulled up a map of the campus, and pointed it out. Mason stood up and pulled out his phone, stepping over to take a photo of the computer screen.

"Can I photograph this document?" he said, waving the bank statement, and when Rovski assented, he set it on the desktop and leaned over it to take a photo, then took a close-up of the balance with the bogus digits, then held it up to the window and photographed the dark spot with the extra layer of paper.

"I'm so glad you can help me," Rovski said, watching him work.

"I'm not sure that I can, but I can do some digging."

He nodded. "That's what I want."

"I need to meet Emily. If I talk to her directly, I might be able to get a sense of what she's up to."

"You can't tell her that you're working for me."

"I understand that," Mason said. "I can approach her for some other reason."

"Pose as a student. You could audit her class."

Mason considered the idea. "That sounds too time-consuming," he said finally. "I'd have to sit there for a month before I could even ask an intelligent question about the subject matter. But maybe I can interview her about something. I used to work in journalism." It was a lofty word for the job he used to do, working on a cheap celebrity scandal rag. But the skill set was the same.

"She's got an inflated ego," Rovski said. "I know she'd love to talk to a journalist. You could tell her you're from *Math Journal*. It covers the human side of our field, not the theoretical questions, so it's not very technical." He turned to a pile of paper on his desk and started to dig through it. "Do you know anything about mathematics?"

"I can usually calculate how much cash I have left on my metro pass."

"That's not math," he said flatly. "It's arithmetic."

Finally he pulled out a thick glossy magazine and handed it to Mason. The cover bore the image of three middle-age men, all of them wearing neckties and one in a tweed jacket, just like the one Rovski wore. They were posing in front of a whiteboard that was covered with numbers and cryptic math symbols, and all three of them were beaming, like they'd just solved the whole thing. The teaser line at the bottom, in hot-pink lettering, read "Luminaries of the Mumbai Science Institute." Mason flipped through the magazine. It wasn't like a typical dry academic journal, as Rovski said, and contained splashy photos and colorful illustrations, but it also had dense columns of lengthy technical exposition interspersed with formulas.

Mason pulled open a spread and read the title of the article aloud: "'Torrid Secrets of *N*-Dimensional Sets and Their Hausdorff Dimensions.'"

Rovski chuckled. "'Their Hausdorff dimensions.' That's so gossipy."

"It might not be technical to you, but I can't pose as someone who works for this rag. Emily would see through me in a hot second." Mason handed Rovski the magazine and nodded to the other side of the office. "Is that her desk?"

"What do your psychic powers of deduction tell you?"

Mason chuckled and walked across the room.

"Maybe you shouldn't," Rovski said, rising and pulling out his phone to glance at it. "Emily might have ended her class by now."

"Put a chair against the door in case she comes in."

"I can't do that," he said, flapping his arms. "It's so suspicious. How could I explain that?"

"Well, stand against the door, then, and slow her down for a few seconds. Just long enough so I can close the drawer and step away."

Rovski sighed but went to the office door, leaning on it and bracing his feet on the floor. "There's nothing important in there. I've looked."

Mason moved Emily's keyboard aside and lifted the blotter. In the space underneath was some flattened food detritus—seeds and desiccated oat flakes—along with a printed card that bore the campus's emergency numbers, and a couple of sticky notes. One had an email address written on it in blue ballpoint, and the other bore four Chinese characters: "之乎者也."

"Does she speak Chinese?" Mason asked, not looking up.

"I've never heard her say that."

"Do you? What about Japanese? They use some of the same characters, don't they?"

"I don't know any Asian languages," he hissed, and Mason glanced up to see that he was fidgeting, his expression pained, clearly uncomfortable to be standing guard.

"Chill," Mason said. "This won't take long."

Pulling out his phone, he photographed each of the sticky notes, then replaced the blotter and the keyboard, sweeping the displaced crumbs and seeds onto the floor and scuffing them under the desk with his shoe. Next he pulled on the top desk drawer, but it was locked. The lower one slid open, and inside he found a deep pile of paper. He sat in Emily's desk chair and started digging. Behind him Rovski huffed and shuffled his feet.

On top were a sheaf of takeout menus—Thai and Middle Eastern and Italian. Below that was a newsprint course catalog for the math department, and then a black notebook. Flipping it open, the pages were all graph paper, and only the first few had been written on, mostly with columns of numbers. He stuffed it into the stack and dug deeper, finding a somber engraved invitation card.

Mason read the name of the event to Rovski. "The African American Leadership Spring Gala. Do you know what that is?"

"It's the black educators' committee. I've heard her talk about it." He gestured impatiently. "That's perfect—you can pose as a reporter from a black magazine."

"I can't pull that off," Mason said, returning the invite to the pile.

"Why not? Spend some time reading the news and you'll be able to talk intelligently about black politics."

"It doesn't work that way. It's the same as trying to fake *Math Journal*. I have no idea what it's like to be black."

Digging deeper, he found a name tag in a plastic sleeve attached to a lanyard:

EMILY

VOLUNTEER

SENSIBLE FRUIT PROJECT

Next to the name of the organization was a logo of a stylized orange tree.

"Do you know about this?" Mason asked, holding it up.

Rovski squinted, too far away to read it. "What does it say?"

"Sensible Fruit Project."

"I've heard of that. They give the fruit from backyard trees to the students. It's like a food bank. I think Emily is involved in it somehow."

"As a volunteer, it seems," Mason said. "This is something I can talk about and not sound like an idiot."

Setting it on the desktop, he photographed it, then put it back in the drawer, arranging the stack to look the way he'd found it. When he pushed the drawer closed, Rovski stepped away from the office door and heaved a sigh, visibly calmer.

"Maybe you can stand there for a minute longer," Mason said. "I want to do a psychic reading of her work space."

Rovski scowled at him. "Is that really necessary?"

"It is. I need quiet—don't speak unless she tries to come in."

"Are you going into a trance?"

"Something like that," he said, and swiveled around to face Emily's desk. With his eyes closed, working to clear his mind, he tuned in to the space around him, and thought of the photo of Emily, her smiling face. He needed to refill his metro card, he remembered, but pushed that mundane thought away, focusing on emptiness.

A tangerine, lush and deep orange. That's just a memory of breakfast, not really an insight, and he swept it away too. The image of the pink horizon at sunset gradually coalesced, the smoky color fading upward into indigo and the darkness of the dome of the sky. Was that an insight, or just the memory of an insight?

Opening his eyes, he got up and repositioned Emily's chair.

"Did you see anything?" Rovski said.

"I'm not sure. I'll get a meeting with her and let you know how it goes."

He nodded. "So I assume you'll prorate your fee according to the length of the meeting? If it's one hour, that's five hundred times one out of twenty-four."

"Are you kidding me?" Mason demanded.

"OK, so a workday is eight hours. Five hundred times one out of eight hours."

"I'm going to be working on this all day— reading and research and psychic work. There's no prorating."

Rovski frowned. "Fine, but we'll reassess your progress tomorrow."

His rates weren't exorbitant, Mason thought, walking up the stairs toward the building's entrance, and he was even working on it in his sleep. Maybe he shouldn't even bother with such a cheapskate. Rovski might even stiff him in the end. He hadn't asked the guy for cash up front because Hanh made the job seem mandatory. That also meant it didn't really matter—regardless of the financial arrangement, Hanh's ask meant he had to stick with it.

Out on the campus again, the sun had cut through the clouds. Mason paused for a minute to peruse the notice board next to the bike rack, plastered with dozens of posters and handbills for events and parties and meetings. Some were hand-lettered, and others contained elaborate line drawings and cartoons, in a riot of colors. Students had such creative energy. Rovski had it good—even though math was dry, it would be inspiring to work in this environment every day.

He unlocked his bicycle and straddled it. Before he set off for the metro, he texted his friend Danny:

Are you at work today? Can I drop by?

As he was wheeling his bike onto the platform at the station, he saw Danny's response:

Here until 6.

Downtown, Mason climbed up out of the ground and cycled the two blocks to Danny's office. One of the tallest buildings in the city, it was hard to miss. He locked his bike to a street sign and went inside. Riding the escalator up, these lower floors looked more like a shopping mall than an office building, and Danny's office faced a light and airy atrium that belied the eighty floors of steel and glass balanced directly overhead.

Danny was a travel agent for Chinese tourists, as Mason understood it, although the company he worked for was branded as a credit card rather than a travel business. A giant rendition of the card was pasted across the glass double doors, and Mason split the image in half when he pulled one of the doors open to step inside. The designer hadn't thought that through—every time someone went in, the card was symbolically cut in half. That was exactly the opposite of what the bankers wanted people to do with their little bits of plastic.

Danny was working alone today, sitting at one of the desks, his office phone cradled to his ear, but he caught sight of Mason and waved. Buff and good-looking, he had thick black hair and an easy smile. Interacting with the public was probably a good job for him, Mason thought, looking over a wall rack of brochures. Even though these were all written in Chinese, their purpose was clear in the glossy photos that depicted local sights, tour buses, and restaurant interiors.

"Mason," Danny called, and rose to greet him when Mason spun around.

"You look busy."

"It's the same old thing," he said, and stretched his arms up over his head, arching his back. "I feel like a life coach—people think it's so dangerous here. They're afraid to walk around alone. 'Push through the fear,' I tell them."

"They might be right. Ned left his car in a garage at LAX and was expecting his gas to get stolen. He was happily surprised to find that it hadn't been."

Danny laughed. "Still, no one needs to be scared of walking around downtown in broad daylight."

"As long as they stay west of Skid Row."

"Yeah, there's that. I outline it with a highlighter on the maps I give out at least a dozen times a day." He grinned and put his hands on his hips. "So I'm thinking this isn't a social call."

Mason took his phone from his pants and found the photo he'd taken of the sticky note under Emily's blotter. "Can you read this?"

Danny peered at the screen. "I think it means nothing. I could ask my mom, but let me check first. There's lots of language stuff online."

"Do you mean it's garbled? Is it even Mandarin?"

"It's totally Mandarin. Just give me a sec." He sat at his desk and spent a moment with his computer, tapping at the keyboard.

"Yeah, it's gibberish," he said finally.

"It is gibberish, or it means gibberish?" Mason said.

Danny looked up at him. "It means gibberish. Like, 'You're talking gibberish, son.' The Chinese like to put things succinctly in four characters— pithy expressions and sayings. Those are four basic characters, something like prepositions, and when you put them together it means 'gobbledygook.'"

"Why would a non-Chinese person write that down and stick it under her desk blotter?"

"No idea, but I don't think a non-Chinese person wrote that. Show me again."

Mason handed him his phone.

"This is the handwriting of a competent native speaker," he said, zooming in on the image.

"How do you pronounce it?"

"*Ji-hu-juh-yeh,*" Danny said.

It didn't resonate with anything Mason had heard before, but he took his phone back and asked Danny to repeat the phrase, thumb-typing it into a note.

"Can you send me the characters in an email?" Mason said. "I'd never be able to type it myself."

"Done," he said, "and I'll send you some links to language sites that might clarify the concept."

"I owe you one," Mason said, tucking his phone away.

"Is it for a case?"

"Correct."

"Well, if the person isn't Chinese, it's definitely an odd thing to keep track of."

Outside again, at the foot of the massive skyscraper, Mason unlocked his bicycle and headed toward his office, passing in front of the central library. He briefly considered going inside to do his research, as he'd been neglecting this favored haunt since he'd found office space nearby. What he needed would be online, though, so he pedaled through the feeling of longing and rode to his building.

Parking his bike in its customary patch of open floor, he sat at his desk and opened his laptop. First he pulled up the photo he'd taken of the other sticky note Emily kept under her blotter, the one with the handwritten email address, and ran a search for it. The results were dozens of pages about Rayborn College. The person associated with the email address had once been the dean of mathematics. So it was just a personal email for a former work colleague—that wasn't useful.

Leaning back in his chair, he mulled over his talk with Rovski. He'd said Emily had a big ego. Maybe he could leverage that. On his computer again, he looked up the Sensible Fruit Project. It had a dedicated website with a sleek layout and candid photos of happy people perusing citrus fruit. The site was beautiful—Rayborn College definitely taught photography and Web design. Emily's name appeared on the page that listed the governing committee members. She was just one of many. It seemed bureaucratic to have governors for something as straightforward as giving away fruit, but maybe that's how academia worked. At least it gave him a reason to approach her as a faux journalist—she was one of the principals in the project.

As he read through the pages, it became clear that it was a worthy endeavor. They convinced tree owners to let students into their yards to pick uncollected fruit, and then they distributed it on campus. The altruism was pure, it seemed, as the college got little benefit except positive publicity and a better-fed student population.

But what kind of media outlet would want to interview these people? Mason spent a while researching legitimate entities that reported on philanthropy, science, and the workings of academia, looking for one that might be relevant. Most of them didn't quite fit, but eventually he came across one that would.

He found Emily's email address on the college website, then pulled up the interface for his bare-bones email account. It used only his first name, with no other contact details, so it wouldn't out him as a psychic investigator or allow anyone to track down his real identity. He composed a message to Emily:

> I'm a freelance journalist and would like to interview you regarding the Sensible Fruit distribution project, and about fruit philanthropy in general. I'm pitching an article to *Citrus Fancier* magazine, and I hope to talk to the organizers of a couple of these groups in Southern California. I'm going to be on your campus tomorrow if you could spare a few minutes.

Reading it over, he cut the part about fruit philanthropy. It sounded way too specific. He also changed *organizers* to *luminaries*. That's what *Math Journal* had called those cover boys from Mumbai. A word like that would definitely massage Emily's ego.

Mason was still at his desk a while later when his phone dinged with an email. Checking it on his computer, he felt his heart pound when he saw that it was from Emily. He clicked open her reply:

> I'd be happy to tell you about the project. I'll be in my office after my first class. It ends at 10:30.

She appended the numbers for the building and for her office—Rovski's office. Smiling at the success, he sent her a brief acknowledgment, then texted Rovski:

> I'm meeting Emily in her office tomorrow at 10:30. Be scarce.

Folding his computer closed, he packed up and shrugged his backpack on. In the elevator on the way down to the street, he read Rovski's reply:

I won't be there. Call me after.

As he walked out to the street, wheeling his bicycle, he felt lighter. Emily had bought it—he was in. Now he just had to ask the right questions.

FIVE

THE RIDE UP THE hill got him breathing hard, and when he stepped into the warmth of the house, the air was heavy with the aroma of food. Ned greeted him from the kitchen, and he saw that Peggy was in there with him, her long brown hair tied behind her neck. She'd changed out of her teacher garb into sweatpants and a pullover, and her apron, tied snugly around her waist, emphasized her wiry frame. Ned was wearing his apron too.

"Look at you two," Mason said, stepping over to the counter. "It smells amazing in here."

"I made ravioli," Peggy said. "Ned's teaching

me his red sauce."

"It's not really mine," Ned said. "It's a solid basic marinara." He leaned across the counter to kiss Mason hello. "We're almost ready. Go wash up."

When he came back to the dining table, the food was already plated, and the three of them sat down to eat. Peggy's homemade pasta, doused with red sauce, was delicate and delicious.

"This is truly exquisite," Mason said, after he'd sampled it.

"So Miss Thing bought a poncho today," Ned said.

Mason grinned and eyed Peggy. "That's a new look for you."

"It's not for me—it's to perform in."

"What does it look like?"

"It's from the Andes, so it's heavy, and the colors are great. I figured it's appropriate for winter. You'll see it tomorrow."

"I'm looking forward to that," Mason said.

"So Ned says you met a new client on the trip home?"

"It's actually getting interesting," Mason said, and told them about Rovski and the case. "You're both sworn to confidentiality, by the way."

"Is that a legal thing?" Ned said. "Psychic-client privilege?"

"You've met the guy. I don't need you gossiping

about him."

"I don't even get what his problem with his office mate is," Peggy said, waving her fork.

"Basically Rovski thinks Emily is plotting to steal from him."

"That's not the only reason you'd forge financial documents," Ned said. "You can create fake collateral, or reduce your tax liability. What's weird is that she's doing it with his paperwork and not her own."

"I'm meeting her tomorrow. Hopefully I'll find out what's going on."

"I'm glad I met Rovski," Ned said. "At least I know he's not trying to get into your pants with this cockamamy story. He doesn't seem like that type."

"That literally never happens," Mason said. "No one ever hits on me."

"You probably just don't notice it," Peggy said, digging into her salad.

"I'm not complaining. It's just a fact."

Ned gestured with his fork. "WeHo guys don't hit on you because they don't know what they're dealing with. WeHo hotness is crafted and honed, but yours is organic."

"Like a thrift store rather than a boutique," Peggy offered.

"Exactly," Ned said. "Plus you already have a smoking-hot boyfriend."

"I guess that explains it," Mason said flatly. "The odd thing about Rovski is that he teaches math. On the plane I thought he was a musician."

"Did he say that he was?" Ned asked.

"He was carrying that violin case."

"I don't recall him having a violin."

"I can't believe you didn't notice that. I remember thinking, of course you wouldn't check something like that, even with its case—it would get smashed to bits. I saw him set it on the counter when he was talking to the gate agent to get rebooked."

"He might have had a violin case," Ned said, frowning. "But I think it would have stuck with me."

"So what was he carrying?" Mason demanded.

"I don't know—a briefcase? A black wheelie bag? Everyone has one of those for the airplane."

"It was a violin case," Mason said firmly.

"I see those every day at school," Peggy said. "Lots of kids are learning the violin. I think it would stand out on an airplane."

Mason sighed and pushed his plate away. "So what's violin music like?" he asked her.

Peggy frowned. "You've heard the violin before."

"Sure, but what's the meaning of it? Symbolically, I mean. What does it represent?"

"You're asking the wrong person. I teach

guitar." She set her fork on her empty plate and added, "Why don't you come to my school, and talk to someone who teaches the violin?"

"That would be super helpful, if you have the time for that."

"Let me set it up," she said.

Ned had made coconut crème brûlée for dessert, and brought out the little ramekins as Mason cleared the dinner plates. When he sat down again, he tapped the shiny mottled surface of the dessert with his spoon until the sugar cracked. Such a satisfying sound it was.

Savoring the sweet contents, Mason said, "So why would someone who's not Chinese keep a sticky note written in Chinese under the blotter on her desk?"

"Do you know what the note says?" Peggy asked.

"It was just the word *gibberish*."

"You're talking about Rovski's office mate?" Ned said. "You looked under her blotter?"

He gestured vaguely with his spoon. "I was doing research."

"Maybe it's a mantra," Peggy said. "Like, remember what not to do in front of a class. Don't spout gibberish; don't babble. I certainly had the jitters about stuff like that when I started teaching."

"Maybe that's the kind of question that can

only be answered by consulting the hidden connections running through the universe," Ned said.

"That's an excellent idea."

"I was being facetious. Why don't you just ask her?"

"It's simpler if I meditate on it."

Ned set his ramekin on the table and took a deep breath. "That doesn't sound like the simplest path."

After they'd cleaned up, Peggy went into her bedroom, and Ned went to his office. Mason stretched out on the sofa and looked at his phone, studying the photo of the handwritten note with the Chinese characters. Closing his eyes, he cleared his mind and focused on the image. Nothing that felt like inspiration came to him, and gradually the regular chatter of his mind intruded.

Hopefully there was more crème brûlée. Ned didn't like to make extra because the crispy sugar crust got soggy if you didn't eat it right away. Mason visualized the ramekins sitting on the shelf in the fridge, but then pushed that away, trying to focus on the Chinese phrase.

But he was too comfortable to remain focused. Drifting into sleep, in the hypnagogic state he was surrounded by floating colors and shapes. The swirling form of a red dragon went by, sleek and serpentine. Is it the Welsh one or the Chinese one, he wondered, trying to stabilize it. He'd have to look that up.

He woke to Ned's hand on his shoulder, and saw his smiling face looming above him.

"You should come to bed."

"There's a red dragon," Mason mumbled.

"Well, it didn't get into the house. At least not that I've seen."

Following him to their bedroom, Mason peeled off his clothes and crawled under the covers, then cuddled with Ned for a minute. As he rapidly sank back toward sleep, he woke with a start. There was work to do tonight. *Herman,* he said to himself. He needed to talk to Herman. Drifting deeper, he remembered the guy's face, and focused on holding onto the image.

Herman was playing the violin, and standing in the same place, at the crest of the hill on a dark street, lit only by moonlight. No one was around—so who had dropped the coins into the case at his feet? The melody from his violin was different this time. Slower. Mason watched as he drew the bow across the strings, watched how his elbow danced in the air with the music. But he didn't want to get lost in it, and he struggled to become lucid, pushing himself into awareness.

There was a tangerine in the violin case along with the smattering of cash. That had been there before. No time had passed, he realized. Maybe he hadn't even been away.

Herman stopped playing, and Mason said, "You're still here."

"And here you are. So what's the verdict—am I real, or am I a figment of your imagination?"

"I checked. I know I'm not making you up."

"That's so edifying. Not that I was especially worried—I already knew that."

"There's a reason we've connected," Mason said. "A reason that I'm here. I'm supposed to help you."

Herman suppressed a smile. "I don't know that I need any help. Plus they don't let the greenhorn climb the rigging."

"Rigging?" Mason frowned. "What are you talking about?"

"How exactly do you propose to help me?"

Mason sighed. He'd hoped Herman would know what needed doing. Finally he gestured to the violin case at his feet.

"You're not making a lot of scratch, for one. There's less than ten bucks in there."

"There's more to life than money, my friend."

That sounded like spin, Mason thought, or the words of someone who had enough money not to have to worry about it. He turned and looked around at the street. Standing a few feet away was a teenager, in a light summer dress, grinning at him.

"Lizzy?" Mason said. "I haven't seen you since high school. You look exactly the same."

"Road trip," she said, and got in behind the wheel of a car, then pushed open the passenger door. Where had that come from?

"Where are we going?"

"Get in," she called to him, impatient.

Mason dutifully walked around to the passenger side and climbed in. "You can drive?" he said, dubious, but she was already accelerating. It was broad daylight now.

"Did you bring the tunes?" she asked.

"I didn't bring anything." The memory of Herman and the violin melody flitted through his mind, along with the idea that he had other things to do, and he started to turn to look back.

"Woo-hoo!" Lizzy shouted, and when Mason looked out the windshield, he saw they were on the PCH, the dark blue Pacific stretching to the horizon, sunlight sparkling on the waves. The car was a convertible now, with the top down. The view really was spectacular. He sat back to enjoy the ride.

Sometime later Lizzy was rounding a corner. It felt like she was going way too fast, about to lose control and fly off the road. Mason tensed up and braced his hands on the dash, then started to scream.

The surge of fear pushed him into wakefulness, into the darkness of his own bedroom. He gazed at the indistinct outlines of the floor mirror and the chair in the corner, reassured by the familiar shapes. The faint ambient light from the city outside meant it was still the middle of the night. The time didn't matter, though, and he forced himself to full consciousness, then clicked on the bedside light, wincing at the sudden glare.

He'd been lucid for a minute, but then lost it. And why had he gone driving up the coast with someone he hadn't even thought of in years? Taking his bedside notepad from the nightstand, he wrote down the details.

Lizzie
PCH

That part probably wasn't significant, because he hadn't been aware, he'd only been reacting. He drew a line across the page and added:

Herman
tangerine
"more to life than money"
same place after 24 hours

If he'd picked up right where he'd left off with Herman, logically that meant dream time wasn't linear. Hanh had said that time was less important there. But how do you disconnect from past and future and maintain any sense of how things are organized?

●●●●●●

WOKEN BY HIS ALARM, Mason climbed out of bed and got dressed. Ned was in his office, and he paused in the doorway, bleary-eyed, to say good morning.

After a pot of espresso, and starting into his second, he was alert enough to focus. As he ate a bowl of fruit, he scanned a couple of articles on his phone from *Citrus Fancier* magazine, and tried to memorize the names of a few varietals so that he could talk about them and sound like he was at least familiar with citrus fruit. The whole field seemed way more complicated than it needed to be, and he worked to retain some of the Latin names.

The weather said it might rain, so he pulled on a jacket and kissed Ned good-bye, then grabbed his backpack and cycled down the hill to the metro. Happily he reached the campus without getting rained on, and parked his bike in the big student rack. Walking into building 12, he trotted down the stairs to Rovski and Emily's office and knocked on the door.

When Emily opened it for him, she was taller than he expected. Her gray suit revealed her athletic build, and he saw that she had changed her hair. It was straight and carefully coiffed, more traditional than in her portrait. That might be a wig, he realized, although it looked real. Ned would know. She also looked a little older without the benefit of a photographer's airbrush.

"Mason," she said, and smiled.

"Correct." He stepped in as she moved aside. "I see there are two names on your door. Is Z. Rovski your assistant?"

Emily chuckled. "I wish. I share the office with another math professor."

"She's not in today?"

"Who knows? And it's a he. He's a bit of an odd duck."

Mason smiled and met her eye. "How so?"

"You really are a journalist," she said, furrowing her brow. "Not that it matters, but he's a secretive type, and suspicious. You know what they say about mathematicians."

"What's that?"

"We're all weirdos."

Mason laughed at that, and followed her to her desk, taking one of the hard-back chairs. Her swivel chair elevated her slightly, he noticed, as he pulled his notepad out of his bag. Even though Mason was tall, he had to look up at her. That was probably intentional, a way to establish the dynamic with the usual office visitors, her students.

"Mason is your family name?" she asked, watching him dig in his bag for a pen.

"First name. My surname is Braithwaite," he said, and instantly regretted it. He should have lied. She'd put him at ease with the chitchat, and he'd slipped up. If she remembered his name, she'd be able to look him up if she wanted to, and figure out who he really was.

"I've met African Americans with that handle," Emily said, "which probably means there were Southern plantation owners called Braithwaite."

"My people have no connection to the South," Mason said, raising his eyebrows. "Although I know that doesn't erase my white privilege."

Emily nodded, a faint smile on her lips. "Do you have a business card?"

He patted his breast pocket as if he might find one there. "I wish I'd remembered. You have my email, though. I can give you my phone number."

"You said you were freelance?"

"That's right. I used to work full-time for magazines, but the industry has contracted significantly. Lower circulation, fewer jobs."

In reality he hadn't been laid off, and the celebrity rag he'd worked for was still going strong. That form of media would never die, as it was closer to marketing than any semblance of information that would actually enlighten the world. He'd quit that job voluntarily to work as a psychic. But he wasn't about to tell her that.

"It's all about crowdsourced content now, it seems," she said.

"And the lack of quality control that goes along with it."

Emily smiled. "Did *Citrus Fancier* commission your article? That would be a big deal."

It wouldn't, not really, Mason thought, absently clicking his pen. He'd never even heard of *Citrus Fancier* before yesterday. Its circulation probably topped out in the low dozens.

"I'm writing it on spec," he said. "I hope they buy it." He lifted the blank top sheet on his pad and pretended to read what was beneath. "So you're in the math faculty, not biology or horticulture."

Emily gestured expansively. "The Sensible Fruit Project isn't academic. Campus volunteers harvest and distribute produce from homeowners who don't bother to pick the fruit or don't have time."

"How does it work, exactly? How do you connect with the homeowners?"

Leaning back in her chair, Emily got into it, happy to talk about something she was interested in, explaining how the project had started and expanded.

"Anyway," she said finally, "The business world already has an optimized food distribution system, and we didn't want to reinvent that. Back-yard fruit can't go into the commercial supply, at least not without getting inspected at a warehouse and all that would entail. Plus they'd throw half of it away for being too delicate. But state laws protect food philanthropy. Our goal is to distribute it to students who are under food stress."

"Is that a lot of your students?" Mason said, looking up from his notes.

"More than you'd think. I can put you in touch with someone who has those numbers. We don't call it a food bank, as that carries a certain stigma about poverty. Instead we have events that we call giveaways once or twice a week during the season, and we try to make them fun and light."

"Can anyone take the fruit?"

"Of course," she said. "There's no means test. Even faculty come to stock up. It's often much better quality than what's available in the supermarket. That stuff is engineered to stay firm on a cross-country truck ride, not for flavor."

"I assume you're mostly dealing with *Citrus sinensis*," Mason said, "but do you run across *C. japonica* in backyards, or *C. maxima*?"

Emily frowned. "I wouldn't know about that. I'm a mathematician. We get donations of what I'd call oranges, lemons, and grapefruits. Once in a blue moon there's some avocados, and even figs and pomegranates."

That was enough questions, he decided, scribbling notes. Now came the hard part—querying her about Rovski's concerns.

"What about you personally?" he said, looking up. "What other projects are you working on?"

"Teaching takes a lot of my time. There are lots of committees, and endless meetings. I work on an African American leadership project. We're mostly academics, but some local businesspeople and politicians participate."

"Do you have any outside business dealings?"

She frowned, concern creeping into her eyes. "Part of my contract with the college is that my attention be focused here."

"That's totally logical," Mason said.

"Do you want to see the fruit giveaway?" she said, holding his gaze. "I assume you heard that there's an event this Saturday."

"I was hoping you'd ask."

"I can introduce you to some of the student volunteers. They're doing the hard work of pulling the fruit out of the trees."

"Where is the giveaway?"

"On campus. Meet me here on Saturday."

As he wrote down the details, Mason could feel her eyes on him.

"Do you play tennis?" Emily said.

He looked up at her. "Not very well."

"I have a court booked for Saturday, right

after the giveaway, and my regular partner just canceled. Do you want to play? The weather's supposed to be a lot better than today."

"Why not?" he said, and clipped his pen to the notepad.

"Bring a racket. The college has lots of tennis balls."

"Is there a dress code?"

"It's not a private club, Mason. It's a public college. Wear whatever you want."

There was a soft knock at the door, and it swung open as a young woman stepped inside.

"Hey, professor," she said, and stopped when she spotted Mason. "I didn't know you were already in a meeting."

"I'm just winding up," Emily said to her, and to Mason, "I have office hours right now. Perhaps you can email me if you have any follow-up questions."

"Thanks for your time," he said, and rose, tucking his notepad into his backpack.

"See you on Saturday," Emily said, and then turned to the student, and greeted her by name.

As he was closing the door, Mason heard her say, "I wanted to talk to you about my grade …"

Slinging on his backpack, Mason headed up the stairs and out onto the campus. That had been mostly futile. What had he expected from her, a spontaneous confession that she was scamming

Rovski? But at least he had a sense now of who Emily was—and there was a plan to meet again.

Building 42, he remembered. Rovski had seen Emily going inside, and he'd considered that unusual. Emily wouldn't be headed there anytime soon, not with that grade-grubbing student in her office. Maybe he could have a look around.

Walking through the campus, the building numbers didn't seem to fall in any discernible order, and some of them had names with no number displayed. Asking someone where the Bunker was might arouse suspicion, so he stopped and pulled out his phone to look at the photo he'd taken of the campus map. Once he was oriented, he realized it was opposite the direction he was headed, so he turned around and walked that way.

The building was hard to miss, he saw, once he was approaching it. The sign beside the entrance said TECHNOLOGY CENTER, and higher up, the windows were narrow slits, like a Gothic fortress or a prison. The nickname "Bunker" definitely suited the place. As he got closer he could see the fine mesh Rovski had described, covering all the glass.

Ahead of him a man was headed toward the entrance, his pace brisk. Trotting to catch up, Mason walked a few paces behind him as he went through the doors. No one stopped the guy, but as he passed the counter just inside, he held up a card, glancing at the guard but not breaking his stride. Mason saw the uniform out of the corner of his eye, but he didn't look, and kept walking.

"Sir," the guard called after him. "Hold up."

Mason ignored that and kept going, but the guy was much louder the second time he hailed him.

"Sir."

He turned back. "Excuse me?"

"Your pass," the guard said, on his feet now.

Mason gestured to the man he'd followed, now halfway down the hall. "I'm with him."

"It doesn't look like that to me. What are you looking for, exactly?"

"Professor Luton-Jones asked me to come over."

He frowned. "What department is that?"

"What's with all the bureaucracy?" Mason demanded. "Let me do my job."

The guard stepped out from behind the counter. Taller than Mason and beefy, he cut an intimidating figure. "If you don't have a pass, you can't come in. And if you don't leave the building, I'm going to call the campus police."

Mason sighed. "Fine. I'll come back with a pass."

What could be happening in there that required that kind of security, he wondered, walking back out into the daylight. The guard wasn't armed, and there wasn't actually a physical barrier, so it still felt like an office building, not a military installation. But that guy had been dead serious. It was probably nothing more interesting than expensive electronics that were easy to walk away with. Still, what was Emily doing in there?

SIX

Walking back toward the rack where he'd parked his bike, he texted Rovski:

Are you around campus?

His response came a moment later:

Not right now. Can I drop by your office in few hours?

Mason's reply was concise:

I'll be there.

It felt like he wasn't making a lot of progress—not with Emily, and definitely not with Hanh's task in the dream state. Before he unlocked his bike, he texted Peggy's boyfriend, Matt:

Are you around today?

Mason had just climbed onto his ride when Matt's answer buzzed in his pocket:

At school. In my office all afternoon.

That wasn't optimal, compared to the ease of meeting Matt near his pad in the Arts District—he'd be riding right past that neighborhood on the metro. Matt taught at a university east of downtown, convenient to three different freeways but irksomely far from any metro line, and sited at the top of a hill. Bus routes went there, of course, but because it was a student destination, he knew he'd watch a dozen buses roll past because the bike racks were full, and wind up cycling the whole way anyway. The only way Mason could get there without becoming a red-faced sweaty mess was on the commuter trains that ran infrequently to the distant exurbs.

It was worth the effort, he decided, as Matt might have some insight. Plus the guy was a fellow psychic, so he could talk frankly with him about all this stuff. Before he set off for the station, he wrote back:

Text me where your office is.

The wait for the commuter line wasn't excessive, as he got to the platform at Union Station by chance just a few minutes before the train pulled out. The first stop was Matt's school, and he wheeled his bike out and climbed on it, pedaling past the gymnasium and the heating plant.

There was a lot less green space here than at Rayborn College, with the buildings much closer together, and there were definitely more people around. But the youthful energy felt the same. Following the directions Matt had texted, he found his building, an airy new-looking structure of white-painted beams and glass. Once he'd locked up his bicycle, he went inside and trotted up the stairs. The plaque on the door told him he'd found the right place:

MATT RIFKIN
ASSOCIATE

When Mason banged on the door, Matt's muffled voice shouted for him to come in, and he pushed his way inside. Matt rose from behind his desk to greet him. Tall and lanky, with scruffy brown hair, he usually looked like he was in need of a shave. His sole concession to assuming the status of a professor was his necktie, its knot loose under his unbuttoned collar. Peggy had probably put that outfit together—the red in the print of the tie coordinated with his maroon-colored dress shirt.

"Great view," Mason said, taking it in. The office wasn't very big but it had a wide window that looked out on the city's hilly suburban neighborhoods, sprawling toward the distant San Gabriel Mountains.

"You've never been here before?"

"First time."

"This vista is mostly about the hospital," Matt said, pointing out the rambling yellow building on the next hilltop.

"Is that on campus?"

"It's not, but that's what most people notice when they come in here. 'Yikes, that's the hospital,' they say. I think it reminds them of their mortality."

"So why does your door call you 'associate'?"

"That's all bullshit semantics. I don't care what they call me, as long as I get paid." He waved to the blue-upholstered chairs in front of his desk. "Sit down."

Mason pulled off his backpack and dropped into a chair. Matt must have a better rapport with his students than Emily and Rovski—this was far more comfortable than the hard-backed seating in their office. On the edge of his desk was a block of acrylic plastic with a green plant embedded within. Mason picked it up and studied it. The flat scaly leaves looked like they were still fresh and alive.

"Liverwort?" Mason said.

"The story of my fucking life."

Mason chuckled and set it down. "It pays the bills, though."

"Sure, but at what cost? I'd hate to think of the number of students that I've bored senseless talking about that stuff."

"So Hanh gave me a job," Mason said.

"Fuck me," he said, and frowned. "Is it an out-of-town type deal?"

Mason knew what he meant—they had both accompanied Hanh on excursions for work. She hadn't taken them out of town, or anywhere physical, but rather out of the present, and back through time. It was easy for her, something that felt like part of her nature, but it was always jarring for Mason, and for Matt too.

"It's about working with a guy in the dream state."

"That woman," Matt said flatly, leaning back in his chair. "At least you can't get stuck there."

"She implied that the dream world is just as valid as this one. That the people you meet there are versions of people from waking reality. Do you buy that?"

"That's actually the way I understand it. Although I don't mess with it—I expend enough fucking effort just to navigate this world."

"It does kind of feel like twice as much work

to be doing stuff while I'm sleeping. But you don't worry about it? I can just leave it on autopilot?"

"Not if the boss told you otherwise," Matt said. "But autopilot is the default, there and in waking life."

"What do you mean?"

Matt waved his arm at the window. "Every fucker out there is sleepwalking. Reacting instead of acting in this life, just like when they're asleep."

"I've been able to get lucid, but I don't think I've achieved much. Although I did find the guy she wanted me to work with. Do you know any tools I can use when I'm there?"

Matt frowned, considering that for a moment. "So you're already in an altered state of consciousness because you're asleep, and then you shift it again to be lucid. Have you heard of the levels of consciousness?"

"Like meditating?"

"More like stepping outside your own ego. The way I saw it described was with a spatial visualization." He rose from his chair and stood with his back to the window. "Where I'm standing now is my waking consciousness, the state where my ego is in charge." He swirled his right hand around in the air beside him. "Over here, just beside me, is an altered level of consciousness." He took a step sideways. "Here, my ego is partly suppressed, and I can be more objective. I can see all the stuff that my ego filters out."

"The hidden connections running through the universe," Mason said. "That sounds like every psychic state I've ever been in."

"Exactly. This level is like our workshop. Even regular people use it without even knowing it, like when they're all chill and listening to music. Don't call it 'psychic,' though, or they'll freak the fuck out. Then next to that"—Matt took another sidestep—"there's another level, farther from my ego. It's harder to get here. But if you can, you see things for what they really are—their fundamental elements. Apparently you can sense the past and the future along with the present."

"I think I've been there too. You and I were with Hanh. When we went to confront that guy at the racetrack."

"I remember," Matt said, his brow furrowing.

"It was confusing to be in that state. It felt kind of raw."

Matt took another step sideways and stood next to the wall. "One more level away is where you can tune into collective stuff. I've never been there, so I don't know what it's like. Beyond that, there's even more. I don't know what you'd find. Maybe you'd turn into a photon or something."

"So it's like getting deeper into your subconscious."

"Not exactly. It's about getting farther away

from the control of your ego. There are other dimensions to it." Matt stepped back to where he'd started. "So this is normal waking consciousness, yeah? One step below this is sleep." He bent his knees into a semi-squat, and paused, and then rose again and stepped sideways. "This is our familiar psychic state, objectivity land. And this"—he squatted again—"is deeper in my subconscious."

"So it's a step away from your ego plus a step deeper."

"Right. It's the place where you can tune in to your other incarnations, and communicate lucidly with them."

"You mean past lives?"

"And concurrent ones," Matt said.

"Other versions," Mason said, and sighed. "Hanh talked about that."

"You can go deeper. The next level down is about experiencing the planet's history. Things like rocks and dinosaurs."

"That might be too much for me. But it's a useful framework."

"They're also not discrete states," Matt said, returning to his chair. "It's a continuum of consciousness. The basic idea is that there are multiple dimensions to it, not just a single path downward into the subconscious."

"I get the advantage to stepping away from

your ego. You can be more objective."

"Plus it lets you do things differently. You know what it feels like when you're in an altered state—you realize how constricting your ego is. We need it to function in the world, but it's inflexible, and it wants to control everything. Like an officious European train conductor with short-male syndrome. It's really just a small part of who you are."

"I think I know that, in some way," Mason said, absorbing it all. The idea resonated, even though he'd never put it into words before. "And the steps are a useful way to visualize it. If I'm able to shift into other states of mind when I'm awake, why not when I'm asleep?"

"Why the fuck not?" Matt said, throwing up his hands.

"I knew you'd have something useful," Mason said, and stood up, pulling his bag on. "Do you want to get lunch?"

"I can't. But I'll see you tonight."

He'd almost forgotten about that—Peggy was performing later. "You will indeed. So is there a cafeteria on campus?"

"There is, but you shouldn't bother. Spare yourself the fucking misery."

Mason grinned. "Good to know," he said, and went down to where he'd parked his bike. The ride to his office was a few miles, but it was mostly downhill. He didn't bother waiting for the train, instead coasting to the boulevard and cycling west toward downtown, across the river and through Chinatown.

On the way he stopped at a Cantonese place and ordered takeout, an entrée of string beans with chili and garlic. The place was busy, he saw, glancing around while he waited, with clientele who looked like they'd be headed back downtown to their offices after lunch.

Up in his own office a few minutes later, as he was sitting at his desk and savoring the string beans, he got a text from Peggy:

> The violin teacher can talk to you here tomorrow morning.

Wiping the brown sauce off his hands, he wrote back:

> Right on. Thanks for setting it up.

She answered a moment later:

> See you tonight.

Mason sent her a thumbs-up, and then rose and threw his food boxes in the trash and washed his hands. The room was redolent of garlic now, and he went over to the controller on the wall to turn up the fan on the heating system. Hopefully that would disperse the smell.

Before he could get back to his desk, there was a knock at the door, and he pulled it open to find Rovski.

"What did you find out?" he asked, stepping inside.

"Have a seat," Mason said. "Do you want a coffee?"

"If you're offering your lovely espresso, I would very much like one."

Mason smiled at that and went to the machine, returning to the sofa a minute later with two small cups, setting them on the coffee table in front of Rovski. Scooping it up, he sipped at it as Mason dropped into the wing chair, glancing briefly at the gray sky outside the windows.

"Emily told me all about giving away fruit," Mason said. "I asked her about her personal life, but she was guarded about that. I didn't get much insight into her nonacademic activities."

"So you've made no progress."

"I'm going to play tennis with her on Saturday."

Rovski's eyebrows shot up. "Why?"

"She asked. Spending some time with her might lead to useful information. We can stop the clock on your fee for tomorrow, and restart it Saturday."

"Fine," he said, and frowned.

"I also tried to get into building 42, but the

guard on the door threw me out. I'm curious to know what she's doing in there."

"There's no connection to the math faculty, I know that."

"Is it possible that she teaches some computer classes in that building?" Mason said. "Software coding isn't far from math."

"I don't think there are any classrooms in the Bunker. It's all research labs. Besides, she's not teaching computers. In academia, you stick to your own field."

"You never thought about teaching music?" Mason said, sipping at his espresso.

"Of course not. I know nothing about music."

"You play the violin."

Rovski laughed. "No, I don't. I took a few piano lessons in my youth, but I'm not musical. Why would you say that?"

"I saw you carrying a violin case."

"No, you didn't," he said slowly.

Watching him, Mason took a slow, deep breath.

"I can't even read music," Rovski said, and set his cup on the table. "Although it's like you said about coding, it's not far away—music is all math. The frequencies of the notes are fractions of one another. Musicians even use mathematical terms. They talk about three-quarter time, and eighth notes."

"So you've never played the violin. You didn't have a violin case with you on the trip back from Ithaca."

"I think I'd remember if I did."

"What does the name Herman mean to you?"

"I don't know anyone with that name." Rovski's eyes narrowed. "Are you confusing me with another client? Or are you in some kind of psychic trance right now?"

"I hope not." It wasn't that Rovski was crazy, or lying, he knew that, even though those were the first explanations that came to mind. Mason wasn't crazy either. Something else was going on.

"Can you ask some of your colleagues about the Bunker?" he said finally. "What kind of lab research is going on in there that might require a mathematician? And how can I get in? I think that's our most likely avenue right now."

Rovski nodded, concern in his eyes. "I'll let you know." He drained his little cup, then got to his feet. Mason walked behind him to the door. Pausing before he left, Rovski spoke gravely. "Take care of yourself."

At his desk, Mason sat for a minute, arms folded, staring absently out the window, lost in thought. When he eventually stirred, he checked the time. It was still a while before he had to go to his shrink appointment, and he pulled open his computer. There was a phrase Hanh had used that he wanted to research: multidimensional personality. Far from being Hanh's own idea, he found, it was an established concept—thousands of results came up, and he scanned some of the pages that felt more promising.

The theory had several variations, but in essence it ran that each person existed as different versions in various historical eras, even in the future, even in parallel universes. Most of the writers talked about back-channel communication that happened among the array of versions that made up the whole self. It sounded something like the idea of reincarnation, but as one writer pointed out, if linear time was just a construct, all the versions existed at the same time rather than as a progression. Another source said that any living person had as many as six other concurrent versions somewhere on the planet.

Mason sat back, absorbing it all. In a way it was burdensome to think that he wasn't unique, that he might have some responsibility to other versions of himself. But it fit with meeting Herman, the dream-world version of Rovski. Maybe it was more palatable that way—Rovski was the multidimensional personality, and he and Herman were part of a job, not something Mason needed to deal with concerning himself.

Thinking about it, Hanh had called Rovski "the violinist," so it wasn't just Mason who had that notion. Maybe she'd meant Herman, and Herman definitely played the instrument. It just wasn't possible that he was mistaken about seeing Rovski with the violin case on the plane. He remembered it too clearly. He could visualize him holding the black case in front of his chest as he pushed past Ned in the narrow aisle.

Time to go, he saw, and took a deep breath, mentally preparing himself, then slung on his backpack. Out to the lobby and into the main stairwell, he walked up one flight, then went to the door of the office that was directly above his own. The sign on it read COME IN, so he slid it over to read PLEASE KNOCK, then stepped inside.

Miss Cassie looked up from her screen and smiled. Her jet-black hair was immaculately coiffed, as it always was, to the point that when Ned met her, he thought it was a wig, explaining that lots of black women wore them. Mason was clueless about things like that, and just took it at face value. Miss Cassie's dark-red tailored suit complemented her curvy frame and made her look younger than her age, which had to be around sixty.

"I'll be right with you," she said, and Mason settled into his usual chair, tucking his bag between his feet. The view through her tall windows was the same as his own, just a little higher, which slightly shifted the perspective. The layout of the room was identical to his, although she had several bookcases, and a big carpet that warmed up the space, and much better furniture. Mason had a long relationship with Miss Cassie, and had worked with her on his first case, when he'd tried to track down her daughter. She'd somehow manipulated him into becoming her client, and later he'd managed to obtain his own office space downstairs in part because he'd been coming here every week.

Miss Cassie joined him on the adjacent sofa, taking a moment to scan her notes on her tablet. She asked him her usual opening questions—How are you sleeping? How's home life? How's your stress level? It was the psychological equivalent of flossing.

Eventually she asked him, "So how is business one flight down?"

"When I first met my new client, he was carrying a violin case," Mason said, "but later, when I mentioned it, he said that he hadn't been, and he'd never played the violin. Ned doesn't remember the violin case either. What do you think that means?"

Miss Cassie raised her eyebrows. "He's lying, or you were mistaken."

"I don't think so. I think I was seeing something about him that wasn't focused in the physical plane."

"Do you often see things that aren't there?"

"It was there, even if no one else saw it. I was able to perceive it."

"So we're back to your special powers," she said.

"It's not just me. Anyone can be psychic. I just did the work to build up that muscle."

"Which means you can see things that no one else can."

"I'm not going to insist that I saw the violin case. I don't want to get locked up on a psychiatric hold." His eyes narrowed. "Is that something you can do—commit someone on a 5150?"

"Not unilaterally. Are you afraid of getting locked up?"

"Of course. I guess my real concern is keeping things straight—knowing what most people perceive and sticking to that. More important to my case, though, the violin has to be significant. What does a violin represent?"

Miss Cassie stifled a sigh as she looked away. "The violin ... to me it implies a connection to the middle ages, and to classical music, and the hard work it takes to master the instrument."

"Interesting," Mason said.

"What does it represent to you?"

"I'm not sure yet. I'm going to talk to a violin teacher tomorrow."

"You said you saw the violin case. Did you see

the actual violin?"

"Such a good point," Mason said, and reached into his backpack to pull out his notepad. He wrote:

> Rovski had the case
> Herman had the violin

"So how did you meet this client?" Miss Cassie asked.

"We were in the East for a couple of days, and this guy was on both our flights back. I actually wrote it down in my coincidence journal. On the second flight I sat beside him, and he was looking for someone to do the kind of work that I do, so it was more than a coincidence."

"An instance of synchronicity."

Mason grinned. "Exactly. I'm so glad you get it." She was usually so skeptical of paranormal stuff.

"Have you read Carl Jung?"

"Not really. I know he was a shrink."

"A founding researcher in the field. He's the one who coined the word *synchronicity*." She set her tablet in her lap and rubbed her temples, closing her eyes. "Since you've been my client, I've read a lot of Jung."

"Right on," Mason said. "He sounds totally tuned in."

"The risk is in looking for synchronicity in

every coincidence," she said, meeting his gaze. "It can become an obsession. You'll always find patterns."

"I'm not doing that. Half the stuff I write down in my journal doesn't have any discernible value."

"But you keep track."

"I have to. It might be important later."

They talked about it some more, and mostly it felt like she was trying to keep him grounded. She had given up trying to get him to see his psychic power as delusional, after many months of prodding, which had deepened his respect for her—it took an open mind to work with a worldview that she didn't believe.

"What do you think of the idea that there are multiple versions of us?" Mason asked her.

"That sounds like a religious belief. Like reincarnation."

"I guess it is. What about in the dream state? Do you think the people you meet there are real? Like they're dreaming too?"

"No," she said flatly. "Back to Jung again, he thought that dreams revealed our collective memories—an echo of the shared human experience. But he didn't think you could interact with other people in your dreams."

"That seems like such a limited understanding of it."

Miss Cassie sighed. "Jung also said that the symbolism in dreams is reflected in mythology. I remember you were reading Ovid. If images like your violin come up in your dreams, you might look for them in myths. Maybe you'll get some clarity."

"That might actually be useful," he said, and wrote it down on his pad.

"Always a pleasure, Mason," she said, glancing at the wall clock.

He tucked his pad into his bag and rose. "Can I use the back stairs?"

"If you must."

He grinned and said, "See you next week."

Walking over to the glass door in the corner, he unlocked the bolt and stepped into the stairwell. The doors were new, installed by the building's owners after Mason had helped uncover the sealed-off stairs and the glowing glass column suspended in the void in the middle. The landlords had agreed it was just too beautiful to leave unseen, the constant light channeled from above just too valuable. As he walked the four short quarter flights to his office, following the spiral of the square staircase downward, he admired the glow in the glass column, smiling at the memory of first finding it.

Above him he heard Miss Cassie flip the deadbolt on her door, and he dug out his keys to unlock his own. As he stepped into his office he felt his phone buzz in his pants. It was a text from Ned:

Dinner early so we can make Peggy's performance.

Mason thumb-typed a reply:

Home in 30.

SEVEN

ALREADY SET OUT ON the dining table when Mason got in were two bowls and forks. Mason pulled off his backpack and greeted Ned as he stepped out of the kitchen.

"Chopped salad with artichoke hearts and capers," Ned announced, and they sat together to eat.

"So where is Peggy playing?" Mason asked, between forkfuls.

"At a raunchy Irish bar on Fairfax. The real question is, which vehicle do we take?"

Mason finished his mouthful before he spoke. "If it's a raunchy bar, it has to be the Barracuda, don't you think?"

"I've been through it a dozen times in my mind, sweets, and I keep coming back to that exact same answer."

He chuckled. "I'm glad you've put some thought into it."

When they'd both finished, Ned rose and carried the empty bowls into the kitchen.

Standing up and stretching, Mason called to him, "What should I wear?"

"Flannel," Ned said flatly.

In the bedroom he pulled on a pair of jeans and found a heavy plaid shirt with long sleeves.

"Perfect," Ned said, walking in and assessing his outfit. "No one will mess with you."

Mason sat on the chair in the corner and chatted with Ned as he changed into a pair of black pants and an olive drab crewneck sweater. Once he was ready, Mason locked the front door as Ned went into the garage, then waited while he backed out the Barracuda. The car was older than Ned was, but he kept every inch of it sparkling like new with regular ritualistic detailing sessions in the driveway.

Mason climbed in the passenger side, feeling the familiar thrum of the throaty engine, and Ned skillfully nosed the car down the hill to the boulevard.

"How's your case going?" Ned asked, craning

to check the traffic as he made the turn.

Mason told him about it, and added, "You were right—Rovski didn't have a violin case with him on those flights. He doesn't even play."

"So why did you think he did?"

"Because I saw it. On the first flight when he pushed past you, then at the gate when we got rebooked, and then he put it in the overhead bin on the flight to LA."

"But he wasn't carrying a violin case," Ned said intently, glancing over at him, his tone belying his calm driving. "I don't want to say you need glasses, but maybe you need glasses."

"That's not what it is. I think I was seeing other aspects of the guy, not just the stuff visible in this reality."

"You realize that's the equivalent of seeing things that aren't there."

"That's what Miss Cassie said."

"Good," Ned said emphatically.

"It's the wrong way to look at it, though. The violin case really was there—somewhere—just not visible."

"But you didn't know that it wasn't real. Your subconscious psychic mind or whatever filled it in. Are you not concerned that you can't tell the difference?"

Mason looked out the window at the dark city rolling by. "I do need to figure that out."

Thinking it through, it seemed odd that reality was so malleable, as his psychic skills progressed, and not fixed enough that he could confidently share it with others. Most people must just learn not to see the deeper information. If he was losing that filter, he definitely needed to get a grip on what the consensus was, and what wasn't part of it. Ned was right—it was something to be concerned about.

Ned found an open curb space on a side street and backed in, looking over his shoulder, his elbow on top of the seat. After he locked up the Barracuda, they walked around the corner to the bar. A clot of smokers stood around on the sidewalk out front, talking in loud voices. One guy gestured wildly with his vape pen as he made his point. Inside the place was louder, and raucous, and many of the clientele were acting intoxicated. Mason could hear live music, and he followed Ned as he weaved his way through the crowd between the tables and the long bar, eventually emerging in the performance space, in a small room at the back.

It wasn't that crowded in front of the little stage, raised to knee height, but there was nowhere to sit, so they stood among the audience and listened to the performer, a guy playing a concertina and wearing a porkpie hat. Rail-thin, he wore suspenders over a white button-up undershirt. Not everyone was focused on the stage, instead engaged in alcohol-fueled conversation, some with their backs to him. But the performer had a mike and amplification, so his little squeeze box set the tone for the room.

Mason leaned close to Ned and raised his voice over the music. "Why are Irish bars always so rough?"

"I don't see it as rough," Ned said. "Just unpretentious."

"Half of the men look like Celtic thugs."

Ned glanced around. "They're not—they're just straight guys. Plus it's not the Irish you have to worry about. It's the Aussies who like to fight."

"Are you OK to be in here with all the boozing?"

"Seeing this craziness reinforces why I don't drink."

"Gilbert thought you needed to be protected from it," Mason said. "As if the beer in the fridge might trigger you, and topple you off the wagon."

"He's learning how to be sensitive, and he's overdoing it a little. It's like people who've just given up smoking—they're the most adamant proselytizers for quitting. Gilbert is newly sensitive, so he's being righteous about it. It's just a phase."

"I hope so."

"In the big picture, it's great that he's working to improve himself."

Across the room he spotted Matt, making his way from the bar. Ned saw him too, and raised a hand to wave him over. Matt's scruffiness fit in with this crowd, and he'd dressed for the venue, in worn jeans and a green army jacket.

"Were you backstage?" Ned asked him.

"I saw Peggy's outfit coming together," Matt said. "It's kind of an ordeal."

"Not for you, though," Mason said.

He grinned. "It's freaking painful to watch. That poncho must weigh eighty pounds. Do you want to get a drink? She won't be on for a while."

"I'll go," Mason said. "What do you want?"

"Soda water," Matt said, and Ned just shook his head.

"What should I get for me?" Mason said. "I'm not going to order a margarita in a place like this."

"Ask for an Irish car bomb," Matt said.

Ned laughed. "That's definitely the thing to order. But have them make it with an IPA."

"What's in it?" Mason said.

Matt threw up his hands. "You'll find out."

Sidestepping and weaving through the clusters of patrons on his way to the bar, Mason finally caught the attention of one of the busy bartenders.

"A soda water, and an Irish car bomb," he said, leaning toward the guy to be heard. "Can you make it with an IPA?"

The bartender nodded and smirked as he stepped away. Mason watched him fill a highball glass from the fountain, then press a lime wedge onto the rim. Next he made the cocktail, starting with a pint of cloudy reddish beer. He dumped a generous pour of whisky into it, and then a shot of some kind of liqueur. After Mason paid the guy, he sipped at the drink. It mostly tasted like beer but with a sweet heady undertone.

Walking back to join Ned and Matt, he held the drinks high to avoid spilling them when he got jostled, eventually reaching the duo and handing Matt his soda water.

"This is good," Mason said, taking another mouthful from his glass.

"Go slow," Ned said. "Those are strong."

"I wish I could get one," Matt said, "but I'm the goddamn driver."

"Have a sip," Mason said, and offered him the glass.

Matt took a drink and handed it back. "It's like mother's milk."

As they chatted, the three of them straining their voices, Mason checked out the crowd and listened to the guy with the concertina. The music was folky and upbeat, and actually enjoyable, considering the genre. Ned shifted his attention to the stage for a while, his head bobbing to the music. Eventually the performer finished his piece and shouted, "Good night." People clapped and hooted for him as he walked off stage.

A woman in a baggy cable-knit sweater appeared from the wings and stepped up to the mike. "Thank you, comrades. Next up is the inimitable Peggy Pregnant."

The crowd clapped as she retreated, and a moment later Peggy walked out, dressed as her Peggy Pregnant persona—a flowered headband over her long straight hair, bell-bottom jeans, and a colorful poncho draped over her massive fake baby bump. She'd found the strap-on belly years ago, at a film-industry prop-house liquidation sale, and had made it part of her act. Tonight she was practically teetering on a pair of high cork wedges as she stepped up to the mike, brandishing her guitar.

"Thank you so much," she said, leaning into the mike and absently strumming a chord. "It's so nice to be here. I wasn't sure if I'd make it with my due date so close."

"Show us you tits," a guy shouted from the back of the room.

Several people groaned, resigned to the harassment that came with the degree of drunkenness pervading the place, but a woman at the side of the room shouted a warning: "Hey!"

"It's OK," Peggy said calmly, holding up a palm. "You probably don't really want to see them right now. There's a yellowy discharge that starts in the fourth trimester." She paused to wince and massage her massive belly. "Plus the veins are getting dark and ropy to support lactation. They're not especially sexy right now."

Looking around, Mason saw that people in the crowd were laughing.

"I'm getting nauseous," Ned said.

His eyes fixed on Peggy, a big goofy smile on his face, Matt said, "That's the point."

Peggy started to play, her fingers confident on the strings, the melody breezy and clear. Mason hadn't heard the song before, but it sounded like one of her own. Her delivery was earnest as she sang, her voice high and pure:

> You're the one who makes me smile
> Not the kind of guy I usually go for
> Seems like I was waiting for you for a while
> But now that you're mine
> Let's get together
> Let's put in the time.

The song had a couple of verses and a chorus. When she finished the last notes, Matt whooped and clapped as hard as he could. More of the crowd had tuned in to watch her, Mason saw, and she got a solid round of applause.

Peggy did three more songs, all of them familiar from her repertoire. It was fun to watch, to hear the confidence in her voice. Matt was flat-out enthralled, his eyes shining, his gaze unwavering. During the applause for the last song, Peggy beamed at the recognition, and finally held up a palm. "Thank you. I'm Peggy Pregnant. Good night."

As Peggy walked off, the woman who'd introduced her stepped out and named the next performer.

Matt clapped Mason on the shoulder. "I'm going backstage. Do you guys want to join?"

"We're going to go," Ned said, and they each gave Matt a bro hug good-bye.

"I'm not going to finish this," Mason said to Ned, hoisting his drink. "We can head out."

Ned nodded assent, and Mason followed him toward the entrance, setting his half-full glass in an empties tub as he went past. Out on the sidewalk it had started to rain a little, but not hard enough to motivate them to hustle to escape from it.

"She's so talented," Mason said, wrapping his arm around Ned's shoulders as they walked. "I love hearing her perform."

"Every one of those songs was her own," he said. "That always blows my mind."

"Drunks aren't her usual demographic, but she definitely knows how to work them."

Ned chuckled. "They can't be any worse than high-school students."

Climbing into the Barracuda, Mason ran a hand through his hair to disperse the raindrops.

"Now I know what an Irish car bomb is," he said. "I've got a bit of a buzz on."

Ned flipped on his headlights and pulled away from the curb. "It's funny that Matt had you order that. It's a pretty intense drink."

"It fit the venue, though. I think it was a vicarious thrill for him to see me drinking it."

They rode in comfortable silence through the dark wet streets. Ned put the wipers on the lowest speed, their muted rhythm enhancing Mason's warm feeling of content.

⬤⬤⬤⬤⬤⬤⬤

WHEN HE CLIMBED INTO bed, Ned was already there, reading a hardback by his bedside light. He set the book aside and caressed Mason's bare chest.

"I can't get enough of your skin," he said. "It's like raspberries and almond milk."

"That does sound tasty," Mason said. "But no biting."

Ned chuckled and climbed up, straddling him. "Are you too buzzed to get busy?"

Mason ran a hand into his luxy hair and pulled him down into a kiss, and they got into it.

Afterward, sexually sated, he sank quickly into the void. He was on a dark street, pushing his bicycle along beside him, gripping the handlebars. Why was the back wheel squeaking? It was irritating, and a sign that something was seriously wrong. Normally he'd never let that happen, would stop in his tracks and pull it apart, or seek the help of a bike mechanic.

Ahead of him on the sidewalk a guy was standing in the pool of light cast below a streetlamp. Seeing Mason, he beckoned to him.

"C'mon," the guy said. "Hustle."

Not lucid, Mason bristled at the command. He wouldn't let Ned or any friend talk to him that way, much less a stranger. Not increasing his pace, he pushed the squeaky bicycle up beside him and stopped.

"Hustle for what?" he demanded, giving him the once-over.

In the dim light Mason could see he had a big nose and shaggy dark hair, and wore suspenders over an undershirt, like the musician at the bar with the concertina.

"I'm here," Mason said, raising his voice.

He cocked his head. "Are you really?"

"Come on—you're looking right at me," he said, flapping his free arm.

"So wake up."

"I am awake," Mason insisted.

"Are you really?" he said, a smile playing on his lips.

Mason considered that, and realized that maybe he wasn't, not really. Focusing on the idea, he managed to pull himself into lucidity, gradually coming to awareness.

"Now I am," he said finally.

The guy nodded. "And here you are."

"Who are you?"

"The name is Hombre."

"Seriously?" Mason said, and frowned. "I've heard enough Spanish to know that means 'man.' It seems kind of grandiose."

"Well, it's my name."

"So you're the hombre."

"Not *the*, just Hombre. Come on—I want to show you something."

He briefly touched Mason's shoulder, and in that moment they were on a pebbly beach, at the edge of the water, all sign of the street gone. It had to be a lake, Mason thought, taking it in. The water wasn't moving very much, not like the ocean. Higher up the beach, looming in the darkness, he could make out the shapes of tall pine trees against the night sky. His bicycle was gone too, he realized. He could probably get it back, but he didn't really need it, especially with that awful squeak. Hombre was still with him, and once Mason had his bearings in the landscape, he focused on the guy.

"It looks like Lake Arrowhead, or Big Bear,"

Mason said.

"Do you see the moon?"

Mason followed his gaze, and found it in the sky over the water, the cool light reflecting below on the wavering surface.

"Waxing gibbous," Hombre said.

Such delightful white light, and so vivid. He could almost make out the rough surface along the terminator, knowing it was pocked with craters. The moon seemed to grow larger as he watched.

"I know what *waxing* is," Mason said. "But what does *gibbous* mean?"

"Larger than the quarter moon, and less than full," Hombre said.

Mason murmured "OK," his gaze fixed on the bright shape. It really was beautiful.

"So the terminator is convex, not concave. When it's concave, it's a crescent moon."

"Thank you, Noah Webster," Mason said flatly.

"That's not my name," he said, turning to Mason. "I already told you, my name is Hombre."

Mason didn't bother to explain himself. The technique Matt had talked about, shifting into another state—maybe that would provide some clarity. Closing his eyes, he imagined stepping sideways, the way Matt had, away from his ego, and then sinking down a level. Standing there, he felt the physical sensation of the movement he was visualizing, like he'd stepped off a curb without noticing it, temporarily off-balance in midair before landing again. When he opened his eyes, he was still on the beach with Hombre, but things looked sharper, brighter, more vivid.

"Why are we doing this?" Mason said, looking at Hombre.

"Can you cover it with your hand?" He held up his palm with his fingers spread, his gaze fixed on Mason.

Looking at Hombre's hand, and then at his eyes, he felt a flicker of recognition, saw something familiar there. This was definitely a more objective state of mind. Hombre held his palm up to the moon, casting the shadow of his hand on his face. Mason tried it too, palm outward, easily blocking the light. All around the periphery now, he could see the moonlight on the rocky beach and reflecting on the ripples in the water.

But why was this important? Time didn't matter so much around here, he reminded himself. Better not to get impatient. Just go with it.

"This is Stella," Hombre said.

Mason dropped his hand and turned to look. There was a woman here now, tall and slender, with a short Afro. The dress she wore was a dark mottled print that looked blue and gray in the moonlight.

"Hello," she said affably.

"*Enchantée*," Mason said, which made Stella laugh.

"Look into her eyes," Hombre said.

"Why?" Mason said. "That seems a little intense for a new acquaintance."

"I think you might already know her."

Mason gazed at Stella, and in a flash of insight he recognized her—this was Emily. Younger, and with different features, but it was her. The Chinese characters written on the note under Emily's blotter popped into his mind.

"*Ji-hu-juh-yeh*," he said, pronouncing it as close as he could get to the way Danny had.

Stella shrugged. "I don't get it."

"I wasn't snooping," Mason said. "Just doing research."

"We've got work to do," she said.

Her words sent a shiver of alarm through him, and then he lost the scene, lost track of his awareness, his altered state of consciousness evaporating, settling back into autopilot. He struggled to find them again, Stella and Hombre and the beach, to reclaim lucidity, but instead he woke up, conscious rather than lucid, lying in his own bed.

Clicking on the bedside lamp, he winced at the sudden harsh light and grabbed hisnotepad.

Hombre, not *the* hombre
one step away, one level down
Stella

"look into her eyes"
version of Emily
work to do

Thinking about it, he'd looked into Hombre's eyes too. Why was that significant? For a moment it fluttered just beyond the edge of his awareness. He screwed his eyes shut to concentrate, to sense the hidden connections. Was it Gilbert? That seemed far-fetched. But next to Hombre he wrote "Gilbert" and drew a box around it.

If Hombre was a version of Gilbert, parts of it clicked—claiming the whole gender like that with his name felt like typical Gilbert puffery. But it seemed so tenuous, and he wasn't connected to this case. Gilbert's life was such a car wreck. How could that guy be organized enough to navigate his subconscious and be there, all focused and functional and doing stuff? He lived in a yellow-tagged building, risking forcible eviction at any given moment, and drove the stupidest oversize gas-guzzling car he could find. And these days his free time was dominated by his alien friends.

Mason clicked off the light and shifted onto his side. Rationally it didn't make any sense, but beneath that, galling though it was, he knew intuitively that his insight had been right—it was Gilbert.

EIGHT

IN THE MORNING MASON walked out to the kitchen, rubbing sleep out of his eyes.

"You're up early," Ned said, looking up in surprise. He was sitting at the counter eating muesli from a bowl.

"I know. It's horrible."

"Sit down—I'll make you an espresso."

Ned stepped into the kitchen and set a bowl and a spoon on the counter. Mason mumbled "Thanks" and poured some muesli into it, dousing it with almond milk. As he munched, Ned fired up the espresso machine, which rumbled and emitted a gentle hiss.

"Run—she's gonna blow," Ned said, raising his voice.

Mason peered at him, making sure he was joking. He didn't really look alarmed, grinning as he worked to press ground coffee into the filter.

"I'm not in any condition to appreciate morning-person humor," he said, gesturing with his spoon.

"You sleep so deeply," Ned said, "and it stays with you for so long. It's like your brain doesn't want to come back."

"What do you know about Big Bear, and Big Bear Lake?"

Ned frowned. "We've been up there. In the summer, remember? This time of year it's all about skiing."

"I mean the lake itself."

"You've seen it. It's a lake. Pine trees, rocks, little beaches. It's pretty straightforward."

"But what does it mean?" Mason said. "What does it represent?"

Ned set the mug of steaming espresso in front of him. "This is why it's so hard to talk to you about your work. My worldview is science, and questions like that are philosophical."

Mason took several sips of the divine black nectar, as much as he could imbibe without burning himself. "Science is great if you're trying to stop a contagious disease outbreak or make a parking structure stand up, but you need philosophical thinking to grapple with the big picture."

"Philosophy can't be tested," Ned said, grabbing his bowl of muesli. "So it's kind of pointless. It's just raw thinking."

"Science and philosophy are different tools for different tasks."

"I'm not buying it. I can read one philosopher and think, 'Wow, yeah, that totally makes sense,' but then I read a different one who's saying exactly the opposite, and that makes perfect sense too. It's easy for them to just make stuff up."

"That seems reductionist. But then that's a scientific specialty."

"Reductionist but true." Ned drank the last of the almond milk from his muesli bowl.

"Philosophy is what keeps things working. Infrastructure for those hidden connections running through the universe that you were talking about."

"Those are your words, not mine." Ned sighed. "Big Bear Lake is a lake. Maybe it represents … a lake. Or it represents water. I've been canoeing up there. It's bloody cold, even in summer, if that means anything."

"What did you feel like on the lake?"

"It's quiet," he said, his brow furrowing thoughtfully. "It's a little isolating, maybe, all that vast open space."

"That's actually helpful," Mason said, gulping at his coffee.

"But it doesn't mean anything."

He leaned across to kiss Ned, then slid off the stool, carrying his mug down to the bedroom.

Rain was likely again today, he saw when he checked the weather, so he put on a rain jacket when he got dressed. Pulling on his backpack and calling good-bye to Ned, he cycled down the hill to the metro, and stood with his bike as he rode the train.

Miss Cassie had said the symbolism in myths paralleled those in the dream world. On his phone he did a search for the mythological meaning of water. There was a lot written on the matter, and a couple of the ideas resonated. One was that a lake or a pond in a myth was symbolic of the subconscious or the inner self. Like deep water, the contents of the subconscious weren't evident from the surface. Other classical tales used the sea to represent impermanence, as the surface was constantly in flux.

The lake where he'd met Hombre and Stella had to be about hidden information. Closing his eyes, he focused on the memory of that place, the quiet surface of the water. The image that came to mind felt more like an imaginative creation than an intuitive insight—gliding across the surface of the lake, like Ned in his canoe, he thought about the dark depths below, the unknown distance to the contours of the bottom.

The implication hit him suddenly: it was about everything that he didn't know. He only understood a small part of reality, not the vast depths of it. His view was only a tiny glimpse of the whole picture. Opening his eyes, he watched glumly as his stop rolled up. It was a dispiriting thought.

After he changed trains, a few stops into South LA, he wheeled his bike out onto the platform and cycled the last mile or so to Hyde Park Collegiate, Peggy's high school. The streets were slick and wet but at least it wasn't raining on him now.

The building was modern and glassy and had a grassy strip running the length of it, lush and vibrant after all the winter's rain. Near the front entrance was a bike rack, the good kind that you could lock the frame to, rather than the low kind for the back tire that wound up mangling the spokes. There were lots of other bicycles but no kids around. It was midmorning, so classes must already be underway. Once he'd parked, he texted Peggy, and a minute later she stepped outside, smiling when she caught sight of him.

Dressed for work, Peggy had her hair tied back and was wearing gray trousers and a billowy blouse. By the light of day her lithe proportions were far from the pregnant persona she created on stage.

"You were amazing last night," Mason said, leaning in to give her an air kiss.

"That bar is fun, but it's a tough crowd."

"I love the way you handled that heckler."

"Drinky Drinkerson. You always get them in that kind of place."

"No one seemed surprised to hear you were in your fourth trimester."

She laughed. "I wasn't sure anyone would pick up on that. Come inside."

Mason walked with her through the halls, lined with colorfully painted lockers, occasionally glimpsing the classrooms full of students through the narrow glass panels in the doors. The place was tidy but the air was perfumed with the musk of teenage bodies.

"It's so wild that you work here," Mason said. "All these kids."

"There's a lot of energy, and teenagers certainly know how to bring the drama. It's the best job I've ever had."

Peggy stepped through an open doorway into a cavernous room that was currently devoid of occupants. A few desks were arrayed at one side, and at the back were a series of long curving platforms, each a few inches higher than the one in front, with rows of chairs and music stands.

Musical instruments were everywhere—several iterations of drums, big brass instruments with intricate tubing, a cello leaning on its stand. Half a dozen violins rested in little stands on a counter along the wall, and there were likely even more instruments inside the black cases, in a variety of shapes and sizes, lined up on the shelves.

"The band room," Mason said.

"We call it the music room. We don't actually have bands. There are a couple string quartets, and ensembles, and of course the school orchestra."

"That's so much fancier than a band."

A woman appeared in the doorway and greeted them. This had to be a teacher—she was about Peggy's age, with her dark hair tucked behind her ears, and despite the cool weather she wore a summery sleeveless blouse.

"Wen-Li," Peggy said. "This is Mason, my roommate."

"I understand you're interested in the violin," she said.

"It's not that I want to learn to play it or anything. I'm just curious about the instrument."

Wen-Li stepped to the side of the room and took a violin from its stand, scooping up the bow. "Have a look," she said, handing the instrument to him.

It was surprisingly light, he found, taking it with both hands and gingerly turning it over.

Peering into the f-holes, he couldn't see anything in the dark interior. He tentatively plucked one of the strings, eliciting a pleasant pure tone, and listened as it gradually faded away.

"Try playing it," Peggy said, and Wen-Li helped him position it under his chin, showed him how to hold the neck, and then handed him the bow.

Mason drew it across the strings, evoking a loud scraping noise.

"Use a bit more pressure," Wen-Li said.

On his next attempt he managed to generate a tone that made the wood resonate, but it was far from a pleasing sound. Afraid that he might damage the instrument, he pulled it from under his chin and handed it back to her.

"It must take a lot of practice to get competent," he said.

"It does," Peggy said, and grinned.

"So you can see how it works, and what it feels like," Wen-Li said. "What else would you like to know?"

"I'm not even sure what my query is. Maybe it's about symbolism. How does the violin fit in …" He stopped himself before he finished the sentence—*fit in to reality?*

"That's an interesting question. It's so versatile that it has become the key component of classical music."

In the doorway a young woman appeared, hesitating at the sight of them.

"Come on in," Peggy called to her.

Wen-Li turned to look, and beckoned her in with the bow. This was definitely a student, from her appearance. She wore her black hair in a pair of puffy bundles, tied with blue ribbons.

"I was going to practice," she said, walking over to them.

"Mason, this is Asha," Wen-Li said. "Maybe Asha can help enlighten you. She studies violin."

"Are you learning to play?" Asha asked him.

"It actually came up in a case."

"Mason does research," Peggy said quickly. "It's part of his work."

"Did someone steal a violin?" Asha said, eyeing him. "Are you a cop?"

"Nothing like that. One of the people I'm working with uses the instrument to busk on the street. It sounds more like folk music when he plays."

Peggy shot him a quizzical look. He hadn't told her about Herman, he realized, only about Rovski.

"How familiar are you with music?" Wen-Li asked him.

"I can't read sheet music, but I learned some of the basics."

"What about technical things like octaves,

and measures, and time signature?"

"I know that good music is always in four-quarter time, and at least a hundred and twenty beats per minute."

Asha laughed. "That's club music."

"Mason always says 'no computers, no music,'" Peggy said.

"Ixnay," he said. "I'd never say that to someone holding a classical instrument."

Peggy frowned. "You say that to me all the time—usually when I'm carrying my guitar."

"There's a more fundamental question," Wen-Li said. "What is music?"

"You mean how is it defined?" Mason said. "I can't answer that. But I bet you two can—you're teaching it."

Peggy looked to Asha and raised her eyebrows. "Any thoughts?"

"One of the definitions I remember from class is that music is a direct tap into an emotional state," Asha said. "Meaning the emotions of the composer or the performer."

"That actually makes sense," Mason said.

"Because music can be written down," Peggy said, "you can experience those emotions later on. We know how people in the Middle Ages felt because we can play their music. It doesn't need to be updated or filtered or interpreted either, like literature or visual art. No matter how old it is, music makes a direct connection to the core of your brain."

"Let me play you something," Wen-Li said, and notched the instrument under her chin.

As she drew the bow across the strings, the sound was startlingly loud. The melody she played was slow, and sad, and he watched her fingers work the strings, the notes wavering as her fingers wobbled. It felt dramatic, even moving, and commanded his full attention.

When she lowered the instrument, Mason said, "I get it. It's emotional."

"What emotions does it evoke for you?" Wen-Li said.

"That's such a teacher question." He pursed his lips. "I guess it's heavy, so sadness."

"I wish they all could be California boys," Asha said flatly.

Mason grinned at her. "What does that mean?"

"The music is more than just simplistic emotions like 'sad,'" she said, waggling her fingers to put air quotes around the word. "The violin can evoke a huge range. Happy and sad are the kitsch emotions, but there's also anger, and surprise, and jealousy. It can be made to sound playful, or hesitant, or alarmed. Fearful, even. They use it that way in the movies."

Mason turned to Wen-Li. "Please give her an A."

"My GPA is already four-point-oh," Asha said, raising her eyebrows.

"We don't actually use those here," Peggy said, eyeing Asha. "But we calculate them for college admissions."

Mason nodded. "So if you saw someone walking through an airport carrying a violin case, what would you think?"

"I'd think she was smart to hold onto it," Wen-Li said. "In the baggage hold it would get destroyed."

"For me I'd know what she does at night and on the weekends," Asha said. "Learning to play well is a huge time investment."

Mason asked them a few more questions, absorbing their insight. Finally he eyed Asha.

"So—are you any good?"

Asha scoffed and took the instrument from Wen-Li, a smirk on her face, clearly relishing the challenge. She played the first few measures of a bright and upbeat classical piece. It was familiar, something Ned had a recording of—one of *The Four Seasons*, he remembered. Mason had no way to tell how skilled she was, except that the notes sounded on key, and crisp, and flawless. He understood what she was talking about now, the wider emotional range, the greater depth. When she finished, she lowered the instrument and met his gaze.

Mason clapped loudly a few times. "I bet it took a lot of hard work to get to that level of skill."

"Young minds are flexible enough to get really good at it," Wen-Li said. "For our generation it's too late. If you start after about age fifteen, it's impossible to become an expert."

"A sobering thought." Mason grinned at Asha. "Next time maybe I'll get to hear the whole piece."

"You will, but it'll be in a concert hall," Asha said, nonchalant. "Or you could buy the album."

"I'll walk you to your bike," Peggy said.

Mason thanked Wen-Li, then followed Peggy to the door.

"That kid is not shy," he said, as they stepped out the front entrance.

"At least she's got the talent to back up the bluster."

"Want to go for lunch?" he asked, pausing at the bike rack. "It's a bit early, but we could beat the rush."

"It might come as a shock to a self-employed person," Peggy said, "but I can't just leave whenever I want to. I have classes."

"Every single day?" Mason said, in mock surprise.

●●●●●●●

CYCLING TO THE METRO, he thought about the music they'd played, and all the emotions Asha had cited. He tried to imagine the violin sounding fearful. Herman's music didn't sound like that, but it fit with Rovski, in a way, and his issues with Emily. In his shoes most people would be angry, or indignant, but Rovski was flat-out afraid of her.

When the train stopped downtown, Mason carried his wheels down the stairs to the lower platform and boarded the train to Hollywood, emerging from the ground again on Sunset Boulevard, and then cycled a few blocks to the strip mall that was home to Hanh's salon. After he locked his wheels to a street sign, he walked to the door under the big sign that said PRETTY NAIL BLOWOUT. He hadn't bothered to call ahead, as he had the feeling Hanh would be around.

"Mr. Mason," the woman on the front counter greeted him. It was an improvement on what she used to call him: "the red man." That was an accurate description of his hair, and probably his countenance most of the time, but he'd heard it all his life, and it always irked him.

Mason greeted her and said, "Is Hanh here?"

"Right now finishing up with a client. Do you want to get started with a cuticle soak?"

"I'll just wait," he said, and turned to the white vinyl sofa in front of her post. A woman was sitting against the wall, engrossed in her phone, so he sat at the opposite end, the cushion hissing as he sank into it. He picked up a worn fashion magazine and flipped through it, then turned to his phone. It wasn't long before Hanh came up to fetch him.

"I can't believe you run this place, given all your other responsibilities," Mason said, following her deeper into the shop, past the half-dozen nail stations and the women working at them.

"I have more time than most people." She stopped in front of an unoccupied station and waggled her fingers. "Show me your hands."

Mason complied, holding out his fingers, which she grasped and looked over.

"I don't think they're too bad," he said. "Maybe just a touch-up?"

"No need. We'll have coffee." Hanh led him through a curtain into the back room, a cramped space with racks of towels and bottled chemicals and other supplies. A table flanked the wall opposite the sink.

Hanh went to the battered coffeemaker perched on the countertop and poured acrid liquid from its carafe into a pair of mugs, handing the one without the chip in it to Mason. They sat on the folding chairs tucked around the table, and Mason took a tentative sip. The java was surprisingly good, considering it had probably been sitting there all morning.

"I don't think I'm getting anywhere with the violinist," he said, setting his mug down.

"Have you found him yet?"

"I did. A couple nights back."

"I only came to see you a few days ago. That means you met him almost right away."

"It wasn't planned. I kind of stumbled across him."

"Are you certain it's the right person?"

"Oh, it's him," Mason said.

"How do you know?"

"Intuitively, I guess? Plus I quizzed him a little, and made him tell me something that I didn't know, so that I could verify I hadn't made him up. It's definitely the violinist."

She grinned at him. "To me it sounds like you're making progress."

"But he doesn't seem to need help. I'm not sure what I'm supposed to be doing with him there."

Hanh wrapped her hands around her mug and held his gaze. "Just finding him took serious skills. Don't underestimate yourself."

"Still, I feel like I don't know what's going on."

"Part of you does. Especially when you're there. You'll know what needs to happen."

"So I need to trust the process."

"Trust yourself," she said emphatically. "How is it going with the violinist here?"

"Better. At least in waking life I know what to do next."

"Well, I'm not directly involved, but I know you're on the right path."

Mason sipped his coffee. He knew better than to ask for an explanation of that. "I wondered if there are any techniques or tools I can be using. Some way to get more clarity."

"Just remember that things aren't linear. Your dream self knows that intuitively."

Her phone chimed, and Hanh pulled it out, answering with a few words of Vietnamese.

"I have a client," she said to Mason, tucking the device away as she rose.

Mason drained his mug and set it by the sink, then walked with her out into the shop. A woman rose from the white sofa when she caught sight of Hanh, eyeing her expectantly.

As he reached the front door, Hanh said to him, "Don't stress out. Just act."

"I'll try," he said, and stepped out into the daylight.

There was a Thai place up the block, and Mason cycled over and sat at the counter, eating spring rolls and curry. He should probably feel bolstered by Hanh's confidence in him, but still, he wished he knew what the hell was going on. Thinking it through, maybe the thing she'd said about it being nonlinear rang true. Everything felt that way in his dreams—lucid but haphazard. Maybe his rational mind was mistaking events in that state as pointless and disorganized. The ego was narrow-minded, Matt had said. Maybe it would all fit together later.

Cycling back to the metro, he carried his bike down the stairs and made the quick trip downtown. Once he was up in his office, pulling off his rain jacket, he saw that the clouds were lighter than yesterday, thinner than this morning even, with the sun poking through. The weather forecast had talked about an atmospheric river from the tropical Pacific, and whenever that happened, the predictions seemed to get way less accurate. He was starting to believe it wasn't going to rain again today.

After he made an espresso, he savored it and stretched out on the cobalt sofa, reading an article on his phone about lucid dreaming, aiming to get a better handle on the technique. It wasn't very informative, mostly reiterating things he already knew how to do, and soon his eyelids were drooping. A loud knock at the door startled him into wakefulness, and he got up. Before he could get to the door, there was another sharp insistent knock.

Pulling it open, he found Rovski, wild-eyed and sweaty, his collar askew under his tweed jacket.

"Where's the fire?" Mason demanded.

"I'm so glad you're here. I didn't want to risk using the telephone."

"Why not?"

"Close the door," he hissed, stepping past him.

As soon as Mason turned around, Rovski pointed a finger at him.

"You told me to change my password."

Mason put his hands on his hips. "So did you?"

"I changed it, and I wrote it down wrong under my blotter, just like you said. Emily tried to get into my account again."

"How do you know she did that?"

"Because now I'm locked out," he cried, flapping his arms. "Too many login attempts. This is your fault."

"Let's sit down," Mason said, and gestured to the sofa. The guy was already agitated—no way was he going to offer him coffee.

Rovski sat on the edge of the sofa, tenting his fingers and tapping them to his lips.

"Is it just your school account," Mason said, dropping into the adjacent chair, "or your personal stuff too?"

"My phone is working fine. I don't think she got into it. But I'm not sure."

The guy was practically panting, and watching him talk, Mason could see beads of sweat glistening on his brow.

"What am I going to do?" Rovski said, throwing up his hands.

"First, we're going to calm down."

Rovski met his gaze, his eyes narrowing. Mason thought he was going to bristle, and push back, like lots of people would when told how to manage their emotions. But not Rovski.

"That's probably a good idea."

"So sit back, and close your eyes," Mason said, and waited while he shifted on the sofa. "Breathe through your nose." He waited a moment to add, "Breathe deeper."

The knot in Rovski's brow started to soften, and his breathing slowed.

"Clear your mind," Mason said. "Focus on nothing."

Rovski took a few breaths, and didn't open his eyes, but asked, "For how long?"

"A minute or two more. Think about how your breath feels going in and out."

Watching him, Mason could see that it was working—Rovski was chilling out. He had to smile. More than just professional concern, he felt warmth for this guy. Perhaps it was because they were getting to know each other subconsciously. After all, Mason had heard a version of him play the violin, had experienced that direct tap into his emotional state, as Asha had described it.

When Rovski finally opened his eyes, they seemed darker. "Thanks for that. I know that deep breathing tricks the vagus nerve into thinking the body is calm, so the mind becomes calm."

"Or maybe focusing your mind on emptiness helps your mind become calm."

"I'll stick with the scientific explanation. How about one of your marvelous espressi?"

Mason got up and went to the machine, tapping the grounds out of the filter into the trash and pressing fresh coffee into it. Rovski followed him over and stood watching as the machine ran through its cycle.

"So what am I going to do?"

Mason poured the steaming black liquid into two little cups and handed one to Rovski, then followed him back to the sofa.

"You have to call your IT department, and tell them you're having password trouble. They'll let you back in."

Rovski sat and closed his eyes, savoring the first sip. "That sounds right."

"Do you have your cell phone?"

"I can't do it that way. It has to be from a phone on campus. It's a security measure."

"So campus is your next stop," Mason said. "The sooner you fix it, the sooner you'll stop freaking out. Did you just come from there?"

"I was at home. I live in West Adams."

That's why he came here, Mason realized. It was on the way to the college, and that neighborhood was a short drive from downtown, even in Friday traffic.

"If you weren't on campus, you didn't actually see Emily at your office."

"I was there this morning. I saw her when I was walking back from a class. She was going into the Bunker again." Rovski sipped at his espresso before he continued. "I spent an hour or so at my desk, doing some grading, and she came in just as I was leaving, acting all friendly and sweet. At home later, I saw the time-stamp for when I got locked out of the system. It was just after I left."

"You'd already written down the bogus password?"

"I did that yesterday. I know it was her," Rovski said, his voice rising. "She saw me leave, and then she tried to break into my account. The password didn't work, so she looked under my blotter and tried more times until she got me locked out."

"So the timing lines up," Mason said. "It's interesting that she tried to use your account right after she went to the Bunker."

"I asked one of my colleagues about that building. He says it's all laboratories and big clean rooms for testing technology."

"So what's Emily's connection to it?"

"You're the detective," Rovski said. "Don't you have a plan to investigate that?"

"I already tried to look around the Bunker. I

couldn't get past the front entrance."

"Surely they thought you were a thief. There's a lot of valuable equipment inside."

"Do you need some special ID to access the building, or just a college ID?"

Rovski shrugged. "I'm not sure."

"You must have a professor's ID," Mason said. "Do you want to try to get us both inside?"

"What if they question me?"

He waved a hand. "You make something up. Tell them, 'I thought I had a meeting here,' then you look at your phone, and say, 'Whoops, I was mistaken. I'm supposed to be next door.'"

Rovski broke into a smile. "That's so devious. It could work. It's also possible they would let me in—there is still some respect for academics."

"So let's do it," Mason said. "You need to get to campus anyway to get your account access straightened out."

"Excellent," Rovski said, and slammed the espresso, setting the cup on the coffee table as he got up.

Mason pulled on his jacket and wheeled his bike toward the door. "Today becomes billable," he said, locking up and following him to the elevators.

Rovski frowned. "Maybe for half a day, or even less. It's already mid-afternoon."

Mason stifled his retort and said, "I want to

take my bike. Should I meet you there?"

"Your bicycle will fit in my car," he said, glancing at it.

NINE

WHEN THEY GOT DOWN to the street, Rovski led him around the corner to a surface lot. Pulling out his keys, he pressed the fob, and Mason saw a boxy green SUV respond with a chirp and a flash of its taillights. Rovski was right—there was plenty of room for his bike in the back, and he lifted it in, positioning it on its left side so the shift mechanism wouldn't get messed up. Slamming the lift gate, Mason climbed into the passenger seat, and Rovski pulled into the traffic.

Rovski was a nervous driver, hunched over the wheel and peering at the road, braking sharply no matter how much warning he had. He navigated onto the freeway, his head snapping left and right when he was planning a lane change. Mason wondered if he'd learned to drive later in life, like what Wen-Li had said about musicians. Maybe people who learned as teenagers were more confident behind the wheel.

At the college Rovski parked in a lot near his office, and Mason pulled his bike out of the back.

"First you should sort out your password issue," Mason said.

"We'll go to my office."

"I don't want to run into Emily."

"She won't be here at this time of day. Classes finish early on Friday. Look around—the campus is almost a ghost town."

It was true, Mason saw, as they walked from the parking lot. There were a few people around, but the paths were much emptier than earlier in the week. Rovski waited for him while he locked his bike to the rack outside his building, and they went inside together, and down the stairs. When Rovski unlocked his office door, Mason stood back in the hallway.

"There's no one here," Rovski called to him, once he'd flipped on the lights.

Mason waited on one of the hard-back chairs while Rovski found the number for IT support and dialed from his desk phone. The technician talked him through it, and got Rovski to read a number from his ID card, and then told him what to type as he stared at the screen, the receiver wedged between his shoulder and his ear.

Finally he said, "Thank you, ma'am. You've helped me so much today." He hung up and turned to Mason. "She fixed it."

"They gave you a new password?"

"I had no choice. She said I had to get a new one."

"Don't write it down."

"I have to, or I won't remember it."

"That's fine," Mason said, "But keep it on your phone or something. Don't put it under your blotter."

Rovski pulled out his cell phone and swiped at it. "Good idea. I can always get to it if it's here."

Mason watched as he thumb-typed and then tucked his phone into his jacket. Lifting the corner of his blotter, he retrieved a yellow sticky note.

"I'll throw this one away."

"Don't do that," Mason said quickly. "Leave it there—if it's the same note, Emily will know it doesn't work, and she won't try to use it again. She also won't think that you're getting suspicious. If the note disappears, she'll think you're on to her."

Rovski hesitated, but then he put the note back. "If you say so, I'll do it. It feels so devious. But I hired you—I have to trust your judgment."

Mason frowned. "It's not devious. It's just logical."

"You have logic for criminal thinking. My logic is for math."

"I don't think planning for human nature is all that different from math. Knowing what people are capable of, you can figure out what they're going to do. It's like solving an equation."

"Math is completely transparent," Rovski said. "People are rash and unpredictable, but pi is always the ratio of the circle, and phi is always *a* plus *b* over *a*."

"You're giving me a migraine," Mason said. "Should we go over to the Bunker?"

"Building 42," Rovski said, and stood up, adjusting the lapels of his jacket. "Leave your backpack. The guards might want to look inside it."

Mason stepped over to the coatrack. "Is this your jacket?"

"It is, but it won't fit you."

"I don't want to wear it," he said flatly, hanging his backpack underneath and draping the jacket over it. "If Emily comes back here, I don't want her to see it."

Walking across the quiet campus toward the Bunker, Mason prepped him for their mission.

"You're the one with the ID, so you have to walk in first, and deal with the guard," he said.

"I'm your intern."

"We don't have those," Rovski said. "That concept comes from the business world, not academia."

"So I'll be your assistant."

"That's much more believable."

Mason eyed him sidelong. "You have to play it cool. Walk in, slow down to show the guard your ID, look him in the face, but then walk away. You want it to appear like you've been in there a dozen times before."

"What if he questions me?"

"Then you have to stop and talk to him. Tell him you have a meeting in the building."

"I remember that part. I say I have a meeting, but then I check my phone, and lo, it's in building 24, not 42. A simple transposition error."

"Lo, indeed," Mason said, and chuckled. "Just act like you're supposed to be there."

Approaching the entryway to the hulking building, Rovski took a few deep breaths and rolled his neck, then pulled out a handkerchief and wiped the sweat off his forehead. Watching him, Mason wasn't sure if he'd be able to pull this off. But once they were inside, Rovski did as he was instructed—paused long enough to flash his ID to the guard's station, and then kept walking. Mason was relieved to see that it was a different guard than the one who'd eighty-sixed him yesterday. The uniform was the same, but this was a woman with dark hair.

"Excuse me," she said, jutting her chin at Mason as he walked past. "Do you have a pass?"

Mason turned back to her counter and made his eyes wide. "I'm with the professor."

Rovski called over his shoulder, "That's my assistant," and kept walking.

Mason turned to follow him, his heart pounding, but the guard didn't stop him. He caught up to Rovski at the end of the corridor, and they turned left into another that joined it. Once they were out of sight of the guard, Rovski wrapped his arm around Mason's back and gave him a squeeze.

"It worked," he said, under his breath. "Such deception."

"You're a natural," Mason said.

"I feel like a criminal. It's so exciting." He exhaled nervously. "Now what?"

"I didn't see a directory, so we'll walk around. We have to act like we know where we're going."

A woman in a white lab coat stepped out of a doorway, briefly glancing at them. Rovski stood up straighter and visibly stiffened, but she ignored them and walked in the opposite direction, heels echoing on the hard floor.

Some of the offices had nameplates, Mason saw: WORKING GROUP D and CCVHP LAB. He glanced behind them to make sure the woman was out of earshot.

"Are any of these names familiar?" Mason said quietly.

"They mean nothing to me."

They came to another junction and turned left. Mason had no idea how big the building was, but by his reckoning, this hallway ran parallel to the one at the front door. As they rounded the corner, they both stopped at the same moment, when they saw the paper sign taped to a door. It was just a temporary marker, a sheet of copier paper printed in big letters:

PHAETHON
NO ADMITTANCE

"I was right," Mason said, cracking a smile. "That's the word you heard Emily say."

"Phaethon," Rovski said slowly, his voice breathy, staring at the sign. "I can't believe it."

Mason eyed him, watching for a moment as Rovski stood there, wide-eyed, mouth agape. This guy was easily mystified. For Mason it wasn't much of a surprise—he'd hoped to find something just like this, a connection to Emily.

Mason heard the sound of footsteps, and turned to listen. They were around the corner, back the way they'd come from, and they were getting closer. Looking around, he saw that a few paces farther along the hall was an open stairwell, leading upward. Mason wrapped his arm around the still catatonic Rovski's shoulder and pulled him onto the stairs, flattening himself against the wall. Rovski climbed a few steps higher and emulated his stance. Mason eyed him and put his finger to his lips. That elicited a scowl—Rovski acted clueless sometimes, but he knew he was supposed to stay quiet.

One set of high-heeled shoes, but two voices, Mason decided, listening intently. Two women. One had a soft voice that was impossible to parse, but the other was clear, and getting louder as they approached. He knew that voice—Emily. Rovski's eyes grew wide. He recognized it too.

"Trust me, I'm not going to take a hit on this," Emily said.

The other woman tittered.

"At least the money's there."

The other voice responded, louder now, but still the words were indistinguishable.

"You can take that up with Lorenzo," Emily said. "That's his responsibility."

The clacking heels paused, then there was the tinkle of a ring of keys, a lock opening, and then the door slamming behind them.

"I thought she was gone for the day," Mason whispered.

"I miscalculated," Rovski said, and raised his eyebrows. "What are we going to do?"

"Wouldn't you love to know what's inside the Phaethon room?"

"Are you saying you want to walk in there after her?"

"We can't. One of them used a key."

"Of course. There's no electronics in this building to open the doors, so it's mechanical locks only. You're so clever to notice things like that."

Not especially clever, Mason thought—it was blatantly obvious. The sound of a key ring, and then a key in a lock. But maybe some of this stuff had become second nature to him. Maybe he was better at this job than he thought he was.

"So the question is, should I just knock on the door?"

"They won't let you in," Rovski said. "The sign they put up says that much."

"Still, someone would open it. I might get a look inside."

"It's almost certainly a laboratory, so you'll just see the anteroom and another door, not the actual workspace. And you might get thrown out again."

They both froze at the sound of the door swinging open, and the clacking of heels walking down the corridor.

"That's Emily," Mason whispered. "Or maybe her friend."

"How do you know that?"

"It's the same pair of shoes, and the same gait."

"Should we follow her?"

"I don't want her to see us together. You go back to your office, and I'll do the tail."

"Good plan," Rovski said, and stepped down a stair.

Mason grabbed his arm. "Just wait until she's out of the building."

"How long will that take?"

"Another few seconds."

Rovski nodded, breathing hard as he waited.

"OK—go now."

Rovski stepped down into the hallway, and Mason waited a minute before he followed. The guard glanced up at him as he passed, but he ignored her and went out into the late-afternoon daylight.

There was no sign of Emily, he realized, scanning the walkways and lawns. There were only a handful of people in view, including Rovski, off in the distance, walking toward his building.

"Damn it," he muttered. He'd waited too long, and he'd lost her. He'd blown it.

Mason set off across campus, and was halfway back when his phone buzzed in his pants. Pulling it out to check, he found a text from Rovski:

> She was in the office changing her shoes. Just left. Gray trousers and bright blue jacket. White tennis shoes.

Quickening his pace, Mason replied with a brief acknowledgment and then scanned the building that housed their office as he approached. There were two ways in—the entrance he could see on this side, and the one on the opposite side by the bike rack. He was either going to run into Emily any second, or she was headed out that way. In a few more paces he realized it had been too long—she must have gone out the other door.

It would be faster to go along the side of the building rather than through it, he decided, and broke into a jog across the grass. Once he was at the other end, the bike rack came into view, and he saw the blue jacket, the gray pants—Emily. Today her hair was pulled back in a tight bun. She was rolling a bicycle out of the rack, and even though he couldn't see much from this distance, it looked like a sporty racing model. Emily swung her leg over it and pedaled away. Her confident stance on the bike and those long, slow strokes implied that she was an experienced cyclist.

Mason hustled to his own wheels and hurriedly unlocked them, climbing on and pedaling after her. Not wanting to lose speed, he paused without braking to reach down and stuff his pant cuff into his sock so that it wouldn't get caught in the chain. Looking up again, Emily was at least a block ahead of him. And how had she already made it to the other side of the boulevard?

Pedaling hard, Mason glanced behind him, and when there was a break in the traffic, he swerved and made the risky dodge across. Hopefully there were no cops with eyes on him right now—he'd definitely get stopped.

The blue jacket was still in view, far ahead, and Mason watched as she whipped onto a side street, moving fast. He was already sweating, and pumped harder on the pedals to catch up. This was the corner, just past the taco stand. Leaning into the turn onto the side street, he scanned the road ahead, but Emily was nowhere in sight. There were storefronts closer to the boulevard, but as he got farther from it, the buildings became low modern industrial spaces, with strips of landscaping out front and hedges to hide the parking. Pedaling as hard as he could, he glanced down each side street, into the driveways, craning to see into the parking lots.

She could have disappeared down any of these streets, or taken her bike into any one of these businesses. Slowing down and pulling a U-turn, he coasted back the way he'd come, still scanning for a glimpse of that blue jacket. He'd lost her.

Mason stopped in the gutter, one foot on the curb, breathing hard. There was a psychic technique he could use, and he closed his eyes, clearing his mind, focusing on the image of her jacket.

It took a minute to calm his mind, working to ignore the blood pounding in his ears. He tried to pull in the information from beyond his awareness, drawing her location toward him. But no insight came.

When his phone buzzed in his pants, rather than struggling to ignore the interruption, he gave up the psychic effort. It was a text from Ned:

Downtown for work. Done here in 40. Dinner out?

Mason thumb-typed his response:

Let's do it. Might bring a friend.

Ned didn't ask for details, but said:

Cool. I'll swing by your office.

Pushing away from the curb, Mason pedaled back toward the campus, moving slower now, his chest still heaving to catch his breath. That woman moved fast.

Once he'd locked up his bike again, he went down to Rovski's office and rapped on the door.

"Did you see her?" Rovski said, pulling it open.

"She's a cyclist. Her bike was parked in the same rack I used."

"I didn't know that. I thought she drove from home." He frowned thoughtfully. "I actually know she drives from home. We've talked about it—complaining about the freeway traffic, and the cost of the faculty parking pass."

"Well, she uses a bike around campus. I followed her on two wheels into an industrial park, but I lost her."

"You look overheated," Rovski said. "I wish I could offer you some water."

Mason waved dismissively. "I'm fine."

"At least we discovered that Phaethon is something real."

"And I'm going to find out what it is." He pulled his backpack out from under the jacket on the coatrack and slung it on. "Listen, do you want to have dinner with Ned and me? I'm meeting him downtown."

Rovski broke into a smile. "What a lovely invitation. I would love to dine with you. I can drive us."

As he loaded his bicycle into Rovski's car again, the daylight was almost gone, the clouds in the west tinted pink and orange. Traffic was heavy on Friday evening, and it took a while to get downtown. Rovski parked in the surface lot near Mason's office, and when they got upstairs and stepped inside, Ned was already there, lounging on the sofa. He was dressed for work, in a sharp royal-blue shirt that revealed his pleasing pecs. His necktie was loose, and he'd pulled his collar open.

While Mason parked his bicycle, Ned rose to greet Rovski, who shook his hand, clasping it in both of his. It seemed a little formal, given the circumstances, but that was Rovski, and it didn't make Ned at all uncomfortable. Ned was so good with people. Watching them interact, Mason admired his affable smile, his effortless connection.

"You have a key to Mason's office?" Rovski said.

"Well, we sleep in the same bed, and we share an office at home," Ned said. "I guess he trusts me enough to let me come in here when he's not around."

"I suppose it might be OK." He glanced around the room, then eyed Mason. "As long as you have a safe."

Ned laughed. "You can check my pockets, but I swear I didn't steal anything."

"Let's go—I'm hungry," Mason said, heading toward the door. "Where are we eating?"

"I thought maybe that vegan pub on Eighth."

Mason held the door for them as they stepped out. "I love that place."

Once they'd boarded the elevator, Rovski said, "Are we taking our cars?"

"It's just a couple of blocks," Ned said. "We'll walk."

The place was busy and boisterous, but they

didn't have to wait long, and got seated in a booth along the wall.

"Are we drinking?" Rovski said, eyeing the beer menu.

Ned handed Mason the menu and said, "I'm not."

When the waitress came by, Ned ordered a lemonade, and Rovski said, "Me too." The beer looked tempting, but Mason wanted to stay sharp, so he asked for water.

"What about food?" she said, glancing up from her pad.

Rovski asked Ned what he should order, and soon the three of them had asked her for variations of the house burger. Ned slid his hand behind Mason's back and eyed Rovski.

"So, professor, I don't see a ring on that finger. Are you single?"

"Now I am, yes," he said, resting his arms on the table, his expression earnest. "I had a girl-friend for a while, but I need some quiet time now."

"Did she break your heart?"

"In a way. But also, it was just so much effort."

"Relationships take work," Mason said.

Rovski nodded. "I had to sleep with one eye open."

"What does that mean?"

He shrugged. "I couldn't trust her."

"She was seeing other people?" Ned asked.

"No—she just wasn't a good person. Sometimes in the night she'd get up and move the pictures around."

"You mean the art on the walls?" Mason said, frowning.

"Exactly. I'd wake up to find the kitchen picture in the bathroom, and the bathroom picture in the hallway."

"Why would she do that?" Ned said.

"Malice. When she left, she stole all my sand."

Ned pursed his lips and nodded, as if he understood perfectly. "That's rough."

Mason eyed Ned. He wasn't going to ask the obvious question, because he knew Mason would.

"What kind of sand?"

"It was my collection," Rovski said. "Sand from beaches all around the world, in little bottles."

"Was it for your job?"

He frowned. "It was for me."

"Why do you collect beach sand?" Mason said.

"Anyone can collect mineral samples, or geodes, or gemstones. Jewelry stores are full of those. Sand is more unique."

"You gather it yourself?" Ned asked.

"Sometimes. Friends and colleagues bring me a little bag of it when they go on vacation. There are beaches everywhere."

"Why did she take it?" Mason said. "I can't

imagine it would have much resale value."

"She wanted to hurt me emotionally." Rovski pressed his mouth into a thin line and held up his palm. "I don't want to talk about her."

Gazing at his spread-out fingers, Mason's memory flashed to Hombre blotting out the moonlight.

"Show me your palm again," he said.

Rovski looked dubious but held it up, and Mason studied the shape.

"Are you a palm reader too?" Rovski said. "Do you see something there? Dark clouds on the horizon, or glittering piles of riches in my future?"

"I don't know how to do that," Mason said. "I was just curious."

This was one of those blurry lines between consensus reality and his own experiences, he realized, and he really didn't want to be acting all weird right now. He flashed Rovski a smile, and then the food arrived, derailing any further queries.

Ned tucked into his burger, savoring a few bites and then setting it down. "How is Mason's research for you going?"

"Expensively," Rovski said, raising his eyebrows.

Mason scoffed and gestured with a french fry. "It was an interesting day. I tailed our target when she left campus."

"On your bike?" Ned said.

"She was cycling too, but I lost her."

"I was surprised by that," Rovski said. "Emily is a middle-aged lady, and not skinny either."

Ned laughed, and Mason sat up to protest.

"She's totally athletic, and she was riding one of those high-tech racing bikes. They cost four grand and weigh three pounds. You can lift them with one finger." He mimed the action, moving his upturned index finger up and down. Both of them were looking at him, unconvinced. "Those things are fast," Mason insisted.

"Car chases are fun," Ned said, "but I'm not sure about a low-speed bicycle chase."

"It wasn't low-speed. That woman was booking."

"Breaking news," Rovski said.

They both looked at him, and Mason said, "What are you talking about?"

"Don't you watch local TV? Whenever there's a car chase, they put 'breaking news' on the screen, with video from the helicopter in the sky. I leave the TV on in the evening just in case. Whenever it happens, I have to watch. It's extremely compelling. Like a video game without a preprogrammed conclusion."

Mason nodded. "A freeway police chase definitely has higher stakes than me pedaling around Rio Bosque after Emily."

"So you teach math," Ned said, picking up his

burger. "Do you have a specialty?"

"Do you know anything about the field?"

"I work with mortgages, but the calculations are done by the actuaries and the bankers. I can usually calculate the tip on a restaurant check."

"Restaurant-check mathematics is a unique field," Rovski said. "It's the one place where reality breaks down."

Ned chuckled. "Two plus two equals three."

"Exactly."

Mason looked from Rovski to Ned, then gestured with the last bit of his burger. "I don't get it."

"That's because you've never been a waiter. When you get large groups, and each person chips in what they think they owe, it always comes up short, and the waitstaff gets screwed out of a tip."

"It's why large parties often have mandatory gratuities," Rovski said.

"So you were a waiter," Mason said.

"In my youth. It's what got me through university. I can't believe you never were."

"I couldn't do that job. I would have broken more crockery than I delivered to the tables."

TEN

AFTER THEY'D SETTLED THE check, they walked back toward Mason's building, and Rovski said good-bye on the sidewalk out front.

"I hope you can learn something useful from Emily tomorrow."

"That's the plan," Mason said. Once Rovski was gone, he asked Ned, "Which car did you bring?"

"The Crown Vic. I found a meter up the block."

That meant his bicycle would fit. Mason went upstairs just long enough to fetch his steed, then wheeled it between them as they walked to where the car was parked. Ned opened the trunk as Mason paused to pull off the front wheel, then positioned the frame in the yawning space. Once they'd both climbed in, Ned checked his side mirror and pulled into the street.

"So Rovski collects sand," Ned said.

"Collecting things with value is so pedestrian. Like the man said, anyone can do that."

"His ex must have hated him. No one would steal your sand except out of spite."

"At least it's environmentally sound. You can dump it anywhere and you wouldn't be littering."

"I guess it fits with being a mathematician. Eccentricity is part of the package."

"That's what Emily told me—mathematicians are weird," Mason said. "Rovski's also not very worldly. I told him some basic stuff like how to hoodwink his office mate, and how to bluster his way past a security guard, and he thinks I'm acting like a syndicate boss."

"Maybe it's because he's foreign."

"I thought of that. It might explain why he's sheltered."

"Where's he from?" Ned said, doing a quick shoulder-check as he accelerated and merged the big vehicle onto the freeway.

"No idea. I thought it was rude to ask."

"Why would that be rude? It's part of his

identity. You can tell that he spoke another language before he learned English."

"But asking the question seems rude. Like, 'Obviously you're not one of us; where are you from?' He's here, and he has a job. That makes him one of us."

"It's a reasonable question."

Mason looked over at him. "Where are you from?"

"That's different," Ned said, and chuckled. "I'm a native speaker. People ask me that question because I have dark skin, so it's totally racist."

"It is, but I don't see the language question as any less biased."

Ned braked as he pulled up to the red light at the bottom of the exit ramp. "Maybe you could ask him what other languages he speaks. That would be a subtler way of finding out his background. Wouldn't it be useful to know if he grew up under some oppressive political regime?"

"He does seem a little paranoid. It actually might inform the work I'm doing for him," Mason said. "Anyway, there's definitely one thing I think we can both agree on: Rovski collects sand."

Ned nodded. "Yep."

Once Ned had parked the Crown Vic in the garage and the bicycle was reassembled, they went into the house, greeted by the soft sound of Peggy's guitar from behind her closed bedroom door. She spent hours at it sometimes, practicing and composing, and it created a relaxed vibe in the house. When she played, Mason always avoided putting on the radio, or his own music, or anything else that would drown it out, instead enjoying it as a warm mellow background.

Ned went into the bedroom, and Mason stretched out on the sofa with his computer. The paper sign taped to that lab door said PHAETHON, and Emily had walked in there with her own key. It had to mean something. He searched for the name along with "Rayborn College." The results that came up first were about the reckless youth Phaethon in the classical tale, and then about the courses at the college that covered mythology. Scrolling through the results didn't reveal anything useful, but a description of a book came up that caught his attention. He got sidetracked reading about it, clicking on several reviews, and a summary, and an interview with the author.

The book's title was *The Stoics Weren't Stoic: How the Ancients Avoided Becoming Emotional Wrecks*, but one of the reviewers explained that it wasn't really about stoicism. The author, Fern Aguilar, was an academic at Rayborn College. That explained why the book had come up in Mason's search, at least. Fern theorized that people in ancient Greece handled their emotions differently than modern people do, and therefore the stories passed down to us can't be interpreted using modern emotional norms.

What would Wen-Li and Asha at Peggy's school say about that, he wondered? They had described the emotional resonance that music provides as a direct link to ancient people. Language and culture changed over time, but it didn't make sense that the way people experienced their emotions had shifted. One of the reviewers took exception to that idea too, writing that emotions were based in human biology, which hadn't changed in the last few thousand years. Mason could read the book himself to get a better picture, of course. But the ideas felt only tangentially related to his case.

Peggy's music had stopped, he realized, and he checked the time, then folded his computer closed and went to bed. Ned had fallen asleep with his bedside light on, one hand still on the novel he'd been reading, splayed open beside him. Mason extracted the book and set it on the night-stand, then killed Ned's lamp before he climbed in on his own side of the bed.

As sleep loomed, he gave himself the suggestion that he would make progress on Hanh's assignment. Not that he had any idea what he was doing, even after talking to her about it. Be lucid, he told himself, as he drifted deeper.

He knew he was on a dock. Lying on his

back, looking up at the moon, there was water not far below him, and all around, but he wasn't too concerned about it. Tugging at the edge of his awareness was the idea that he was supposed to be doing something. It was about taking action, he decided, rather than reacting, and then it gradually became clearer—he needed to get lucid. Like swimming up to the surface, he gradually came to awareness, and then sat up, leaning back on his hands and looking around. He'd been here before, he realized, with Hombre. They'd stood right over there on the beach by the trees.

A figure was walking up the dock, confident in her pace, getting closer. Wearing trousers and a summery blouse, her hair was in a short Afro—Stella, the woman Hombre had introduced him to.

"*Hola,* traveler," she said, stopping a few steps from him.

"You said we had work to do. What's going on?"

"I was wondering about that too. My surmise is that we're both here for a reason."

"I certainly don't know what it is," Mason said, waving a hand. "Do you?"

"We're both reasonable people. I'm sure we can figure it out."

Then he remembered. "Do you know the violinist?"

"I don't think so," Stella said.

"So you're not trying to jack his stuff, or mess with him?"

Her eyes narrowed. "Why would you say that?"

"I'm not sure. It might be connected to why I'm here. I know it sounds like something that's not especially reasonable."

"I guess it depends on the circumstances."

Mason's mind started to drift, wondering what her connection to Herman was if she didn't even know him. But Stella's words interrupted his thoughts.

"Maybe we need to focus."

Mason got to his feet, and spent a moment visualizing Matt's technique, stepping into another level of consciousness. He could feel it happening, like the air around him was getting denser, the dock beneath his feet more solid, the fibers in its wooden planks bound more tightly together. The shift gave him clarity. He saw now that this wasn't about Herman—at least not directly.

"Forget about linear thinking," he said, "and past and future, and causality."

"I was thinking more about focusing on what we're doing here," she said. "What's your sense of it?"

He looked out at the dark expanse of water. "Well, for starters, we're on Big Bear Lake."

"How do you know its name?"

"Just a guess."

"I'm not sure the name is important. To simplify things, let's just say we're on a lake."

"You're good at this focusing thing," he said. "Winnow out the useless details. We're on a lake. What do you do on a lake?"

"The water's calm," she said, gazing at it. "We could swim."

"It's also extremely cold."

"I don't like the sound of that." She looked around. "We're on a dock."

"Docks are for boats," Mason said.

She broke into a smile, and gestured behind him. Sure enough, when he turned to look, a boat was moored there. It was flat-bottomed, and bigger than a canoe. A little daysailer. He hadn't noticed that before.

Boats had names, he remembered, and he looked for it on the prow. Instead of words there were two jagged lines. It was one of the symbols from the Western zodiac, but he couldn't remember which sign it represented. Astrology didn't come up much in his work—he wasn't that kind of psychic. But he could look it up later.

"Remember that," he said softly.

"Remember what?"

"The name of the boat."

"Such a taxonomist," Stella said. "Does it really matter?"

"It has a name for a reason. It's inscribed right there for a reason."

"I think we need to take it out, don't you?"

He sighed. "Actions rather than reactions."

"Actions rather than words. I'll take the tiller." Stella climbed down into the stern.

It looked stable enough, he decided, watching her, and stepped into the bow. He got that odd unsteady sensation of being on the water—not entirely unfamiliar, but still a little disconcerting. It was stabler if you kept your center of gravity low, he remembered, and dropped down to sit on the thwart.

"You're the one who has to cast off," Stella said.

The mooring line was at his end, he saw, and he reached for the rope, pulling it off the post and dropping it into the bottom of the boat. Slowly they started to drift.

"It's dark," Mason said. "How are we going to navigate?"

"There are lines."

"There are," he said, remembering. Of course there were; he'd seen them himself in one of the shifted states. Myriad invisible lines running through the world, crisscrossing it, like a rubber-band ball. "So you can see them?"

"I can't, but maybe I can intuit them. That's why I took the tiller."

"How do you do that?" he said, watching the dock moving farther away. There actually were waves on the surface, he saw, now that they were on the open water, but they were small.

"Indigenous people say they can sense the spirit in the lines. For me it's more like I open my mind and one route becomes clearer than all the others."

"That makes perfect sense to me," Mason said. "It's the way I do things too. Clear-minded."

"Clear-minded, or empty-headed?"

He turned to look back at her, sitting there sideways with one hand on the tiller. She was grinning at him.

"Funny. You sound like my boyfriend," Mason said, and turned back to the water.

It looked black and viscous in the darkness, thicker than water. He thought about how deep it was, how far down it went.

"It's a little scary to be so far from the dock," Stella said.

Mason felt it now too, now that she'd said it. They were a long way from shore. But he didn't get pulled into the feeling, instead pushing himself to overcome it, swallow it.

"That feeling is irrational," he said flatly.

"I believe you."

"Shouldn't we be navigating right now? Following the lines rather than drifting?"

"We're going to need power. You should hoist the sail."

"What sail?" Mason demanded, looking back at her, but then he saw it, a big canvas sheet in loose folds at the bottom of the mast, right behind him. Had it been there all along? Looking it over, he said, "I have no idea how to do this."

"Our people have been sailing for twelve thousand years. It's in your muscle memory."

"What do you mean, 'our people'?"

"People in our world," she said. "The whole damn planet is covered with oceans. Just tune into it—it's in there."

Matt had talked about accessing collective ideas in another level of consciousness, just a step away from where he was. Focusing on that, he realized Stella was right—he knew how to do this. Sailing was as much common sense as a skill to be learned. He moved behind the mast and found the rope, then pulled on it, hand over hand, until the sail started to rise. As the wind caught the canvas, he found the outhaul with his other hand and stabilized the boom, and the boat started to move, slowly at first, and then picking up speed. The dock receded and then dwindled away in the darkness.

Stella adjusted the tiller as the sail pushed them forward, keeping the boat on tack. The wind was stable enough, he saw, that he could tie off the outhaul. But first the halyard. How did he know it was called that, he wondered, as he deftly wound the rope around the cleat, leaving it in a hitch knot.

That's all there was to it, he thought, and sat up again, gazing out across the dark water.

"Why is it always night here?" he said. "Every fricking time."

"I'd say that's on you, and your beliefs," Stella said. "You must think this place is in the dark embrace of Hypnos."

Mason scoffed, considering that. "I met someone who went to his house once. It's in Lincoln County, Nevada."

"You're a taxonomist, and a literalist," she said, and chuckled.

"Maybe I am."

"Maybe it's always night because your inner self wants a change from the perpetual sunshine of your city."

"Isn't it your city too?" Mason said.

"Not the place you come from."

"It's not really my city either. I'm just occupying a few square feet of it for a while." He watched the dark water slipping past. "We have nights, and rain, but it's true, there is a lot of sun. Even in winter everybody's yanged out all the time."

The sail fluttered, drawing his attention, and

he adjusted the outhaul, working with the wind. Mostly the journey was about what Stella was doing with the tiller, but he helped keep the course steady.

Looming out of the dark ahead of them came the shoreline, approaching fast, and Mason braced himself for the landing. The boat lurched as the keel struck gravel. He quickly untied the halyard, glad he'd used an eight hitch, as it instantly came loose and dropped the sail.

Stella was already knee-deep in the lake, wading to shore. Mason hopped out, the shock of the cold water on his calves making him gasp, and followed her up the beach. Under one arm she carried a bulky white bundle.

"Is that the sail?" he asked, but she didn't respond, focused on trudging to the shore. When Mason looked back, the boat had become an indistinct gray shape in the night.

They walked up the pebbly beach into a grass-covered meadow, fringed by towering pine trees outlined against the starry sky. Stella dropped her bundle on the grass.

"Help me out," she said, and started to fold open the heavy fabric.

Mason grabbed an edge and pulled it away from her, walking backward. Eventually they had unfolded it all, spreading the canvas on the ground. Almost round in shape, it was huge—the size of his garage—and looked white in the moonlight.

"Let's chill for a minute," Stella said, walking to the center of the sheet.

"Is that really what we should be doing right now?"

"Have you got somewhere else to be?"

"Good point."

He walked into the middle and sat, then stretched out on the canvas. The grass underneath made it soft and comfortable. Stella lay with her head near his, her feet in the opposite direction.

"So many stars," she said. "Do you know any of their names?"

"I don't," Mason said, gazing at the dazzling array. "But I know that's called the gibbous moon."

••••••••

WAKING TO HIS ALARM, Mason lay there for a minute, remembering the experience on the lake. It was vivid, like a memory, not slipping away like a regular dream. But in the clear light of day it didn't feel like he'd achieved anything, crossing the water and then lying around stargazing.

Taking a deep breath to prepare for the shock of the cold air, he climbed out of bed and pulled on a sweatshirt and boxer shorts. Peggy was gone but Ned was at his desk, and Mason greeted him on the way to the kitchen, where he started the espresso machine and then had some oatmeal and fruit. Once he was adequately caffeinated, he went back to the bedroom and pulled on a plaid button-up shirt, then stepped into the office.

"I'm playing tennis today," Mason said. "Can I wear this?"

Ned looked up from his computer screen. Concern clouded his face.

"Absolutely not."

Rising from his desk, he put a hand on Mason's shoulder and steered him back to the bedroom, where he dug through Mason's clothes.

"This one," he said finally, holding up a white polo shirt.

"I can't wear white. I'll get schmutz all over it."

"It's the only shirt you have that works for tennis," Ned said firmly.

"Emily said there's no dress code."

"Still, you need to look the part." He dug through another drawer and pulled out a pair of muted-green shorts. "And wear those green tennis shoes."

Ned left, and Mason hesitated before he pulled off the plaid shirt. It was for work, and Ned was right, he needed to look the part. Once he was dressed, he stopped in the office and did a twirl in front of Ned's desk.

"You look like a hundred bucks," Ned said, assessing the outfit.

"Such high praise."

"Seriously, though, it's great. When you wear white, your skin looks much less pasty."

Mason frowned. "That's so sweet of you to say. You're going to give me a swelled head."

Ned couldn't help but laugh. "You know I love you."

"Can I borrow your tennis racket?"

"It's in the garage," Ned said, and waved him over for a kiss good-bye.

Mason pulled on his backpack and went out to find the racket hanging on the garage wall, amid the baseball gear and camping equipment. He tested the strings and found they were still taut, then shoved the head into his backpack, leaving the handle poking out. There was no risk of losing it, but he pulled the drawstring tight anyway to stabilize it. As he made the knot his mind flashed to the rigging for the sail on the boat with Stella, remembering how he'd manipulated it to catch the wind. He'd known how to do it, and even what the lines were called. What were the names? He stood there for a moment trying to remember. The image was still vivid, but the words had faded away.

As he coasted down the hill on his bike, the air felt cold through the sheer fabric of the polo shirt. At least the sun was out, so he knew he'd warm up by the time he got to the metro.

ELEVEN

AT RAYBORN COLLEGE, MASON parked his bike in the rack outside Emily's building, then went inside and down to her office, rapping on the door. Emily smiled when she pulled it open, dressed for Saturday in a pale-blue athletic shirt and a little black skirt with leggings underneath.

"Are you ready for some fruit?" she said, stepping back to her desk to pull her bulky handbag onto her shoulder.

"You know it."

Waiting while she locked the door, he felt instantly at ease with her, the ice already broken, like he knew her better than he actually did. The reason was no mystery—she wasn't really a stranger, as they'd collaborated on the daysailer, skillfully navigating across the lake.

As they walked across the campus, Emily spoke about the Sensible Fruit Project, gesturing to emphasize her words. "It started when one of the professors in the graphic design department realized that all the grapefruits on her tree were going to waste. The possums clean them up when they hit the ground, but rotting fruit attracts rats too. Anyway, she recruited some students to come over and snag them all, and they put it on display, on a table outside the bookstore. It snowballed and became a whole thing."

"Do you know what cultivar that first tree was?" Mason said. It was an inane question, but he wanted to sound like he really did have the chops to write for *Citrus Fancier*.

Emily frowned. "Taxonomy is not in my wheelhouse."

"That's such a funny expression," he said, and chuckled. "A wheelhouse is on a ship. Did you ever learn how to sail?"

"I prefer sports where you actually break a sweat. Sailing seems like golf to me—too sedentary, and boring."

"Our people have been sailing for twelve thousand years."

She looked at him sidelong. "Lucky for me, there's been an exponential expansion of recreational opportunities in that same time frame."

They came to the fruit distribution event, on the lawn outside the bookstore. A dozen people were hanging around a pair of long folding tables that had been set up on the grass. The foam-board sign hanging off the end of one read SENSIBLE FRUIT PROJECT. It didn't feel perfunctory, like he imagined a food bank would. The energy around the tables was upbeat and social, the students chatting with one another, laughing and lingering. The only thing that distinguished the staff from the recipients was the tags they wore that said VOLUNTEER. Several flat plastic crates of citrus fruit sat on the tables, and some of it was getting eaten right here, with trash bins nearby for the peels.

As Emily approached, a young woman greeted her deferentially, calling her "professor." On a lanyard around her neck she wore a tag that said JEN and VOLUNTEER, like the one he'd found in Emily's desk.

"How are the tangerines today?" Emily said, selecting one from a crate.

"Divine. It's been so wet this year, plus they're at peak ripeness right now."

"You should taste one," Emily said, eyeing Mason. "You can peel them by hand, but it's faster to cut them. Let me see if I can scare up a knife."

"I've got one," he said, and pulled off his back-pack, digging in a side pocket for his penknife. He folded it open and handed it to her.

"The man came prepared," she said, and deftly cut the tangerine into four wedges, handing one to him.

Mason stepped back and leaned over the grass before he bit into it, so as not to dribble the juice on his pristine white shirt. Jen was right—it was beyond delicious.

"That's perhaps the best tangerine I've ever tasted," he said, tossing the peel into one of the trash bins.

"It's all about the backyard trees, man," Jen said. "This stuff is better than factory-grown food any day."

"Mason, this is Jen," Emily said. "Mason is a journalist who's writing about the project. He might want to interview you."

"I can give you my email," Jen said.

Mason pulled out his phone and said, "Hit me."

He was never going to contact her, but for appearances he thumb-typed "Jen" and "Sensible Fruit Project" into his contact list. Now was the time to ask some journalist-sounding questions, he realized.

"How did you get involved in the project?" he

asked her, sliding his phone back into the pocket of his shorts.

"I'm a student here," she said, holding his gaze and getting into it. Mason nodded as he listened, and ate another wedge of tangerine.

Someone with a query pulled Jen's attention away, and Emily handed Mason his penknife.

"Can I take another one?" he asked.

Emily scoffed. "That's what they're here for. Take as many as you want."

Mason took a tangerine and cut it into wedges, holding it away from his shirt. *Citrus tangerina,* he remembered from his research. They were such a rich, beautiful color, more orange than a regular orange. He'd noticed that about the tangerine in Herman's violin case, sitting there amid the shiny coins on the dark-blue lining. Did it mean anything? As he leaned over to eat the wedges, he eyed a whole tangerine sitting alone on the table-top. Maybe it was like an anchor point, connecting here and there.

After he ditched the peels, he dried his hands on his pants and spoke to Jen.

"Would it be piggy if I took six of those?"

"Not at all," she said, and helped him load them into his backpack, selecting them for him and throwing in two extra.

Emily caught his eye and tapped her wrist. "Time for me to smoke you on the tennis court."

Mason slung on his now much bulkier backpack and thanked Jen.

"You sound like a competitive player," he said to Emily as they walked away. "I have to warn you, I'm just a tyro."

"That's less fun than beating someone who's good at it, but it's still fun."

In the daylight, as they walked toward the athletic facilities, he could see that she had serious leg musculature. That wasn't from tennis—she must cycle a lot. It wasn't embarrassing that he hadn't been able to keep pace with her, even though he'd felt that way talking about it at dinner last night. He'd like to see Ned try to catch up to her on that racing bike, or Rovski.

The tennis courts were surfaced in red artificial clay that was so flawless and clean that it had to be new. It was warmer here in the open, away from the lawns, and the sunshine felt great after all the rain. People who looked to be students were already playing on several of the adjacent courts, generating a background of their easy banter and the continual distinctive *thock* of taut racket strings striking tennis balls.

Emily opened the gate to an empty court, and Mason followed her along the net to the bench at the opposite side, where they deposited their bags. A basket of vivid chartreuse-colored balls sat against the fence at either end. Emily spent a few minutes stretching and warming up, which seemed like a good idea; Mason followed her example.

"You serve," Emily said, whiffing her racket around and walking toward the other end of the court.

Mason walked to his end to grab a ball and then stood at the baseline, watching where she positioned herself. Throwing the ball up, he slammed it hard, aiming for the service line and as far from her as possible. Emily dived for it but missed.

"That was in," Mason said.

"What happened to the tyro?" she demanded.

"I guess my serve is OK sometimes."

They hit the ball around to warm up, and Emily didn't hesitate to make him run for it. He did the same for her, but she managed to snag them much more often.

After a few rounds Emily paused and stood with her hands on her hips, panting. "You play like my grandmother."

"That's not too surprising," Mason said, raising his eyebrows. "She actually gave me a few pointers when I saw her last night."

"Oh," she exclaimed, and visibly recoiled, then laughed. "He can even bring the smack talk. You know, my grandmother actually uses a red rinse that turns her nappy gray hair about the same color as yours."

"She sounds quite fashionable."

"Time for a game. You can serve."

Mason twirled his racket as he walked back to grab a ball, then stood at the baseline to serve. Emily won the game, although he managed to score a couple of points. His performance wasn't as bad as he'd anticipated it might be, considering how long it had been since he'd played. Tennis must be a muscle memory, like Stella had said about sailing.

As they played, he looked for correspondence between Emily and Stella. There wasn't a close resemblance, although some of their mannerisms overlapped. But maybe he was conceptualizing it wrong—he was looking for signs that they were related, but the nature of the phenomenon was different. They were separate versions, not siblings.

On the third match, Emily called "Game point." Mason dived for the ball but missed, eliciting a celebratory cackle and a "Yes!" from her.

"Want to take a break?" he asked.

They sat together on the bench beside the net. Emily pulled open her bag and fished out an aluminum water bottle, then guzzled from it.

"So when will you pitch the article to *Citrus Fancier*?"

"Once I write it," he said, leaning back against

the chain-link fence that bounded the court. "Probably in a few weeks. What do you know about ley lines?"

"I've never heard of that. 'Lay' like 'flat'?"

Mason spelled the word. "They're invisible lines running through the earth. Meaningful events and places tend to line up along them."

"Like an occult thing?"

"Sure, or a psychic thing."

She frowned. "And that's related to fruit trees?"

"I don't think so."

"So you're just pondering ley lines while you're playing tennis? Your mind works in unusual ways."

From the bemused expression on her face, Emily didn't think that was a bad thing. She was at ease with him, not dubious, not guarded. Mason felt it too, the familiarity. Collaborating with her and slamming tennis balls at each other was building an affinity.

"Can I borrow your knife?" she said.

Mason pulled it out of his backpack and handed it over, watching as she cut up a tangerine. Inside her bag, splayed open on the red clay at her feet, he could see a little gold box glinting in the sunlight. Embossed on it were two jagged lines—an astrological symbol. He'd forgotten about that—the same symbol had been written on the prow of the daysailer.

Emily offered him a slice of tangerine, and he

took it, leaning forward to eat it over the ground. They each ate another, then Emily rose and waggled her fingers for the peels.

"I'll find the trash," she said, and strolled across the court toward the gate.

Once she was out of sight, Mason picked up the little gold box. It felt sleazy to be digging in someone else's personal stuff, and it was definitely a violation of her trust, but that symbol had to be important, had to mean something, and he pushed aside his distaste.

Examining the box, it was oblong, about the size of his penknife. There was no other writing on it apart from the jagged symbol. A seam ran around the middle. When he pulled on the ends, it slowly came apart.

Lipstick, he realized, peering into it. Twisting the case made it slide out, and he cranked the waxy cylinder all the way up, studying the color in the sunlight. It was a rich orangey-red. Had Emily been wearing this?

Behind him, Emily's voice said, "Do you want to try it? It might work with your complexion."

Mason snapped upright, fumbling the lipstick but snatching at it instinctively so that it wouldn't fall on the ground. He'd grabbed the product end, not the case, and now there was sticky lipstick mushed onto his fingers.

When he turned to look, Emily was stepping

through the gate on this side of the court. Why would she do that, come back a different way than she'd gone? But it was his own fault, not considering the possibility that there were two ways to get in. Why hadn't he noticed?

"I'm sorry—I've messed it up," he said, holding it out. "I know this stuff is expensive."

Emily sat with him and plucked the tube from his palm. "It's still useable. I can clean it up with a brush." She cranked the column down until just the tip was protruding, and offered it to him. "I don't know if it goes with your skin tone, but it matches your hair."

"I don't actually wear lipstick," he said. "Your bag was open, and the gold case caught the sunlight. I was curious about the symbol on the container."

Emily pushed the lid on and rubbed her thumb over the jagged character. "Aquarius. That's my sign. It's a range of shades formulated specially for us Aquarians."

"That's a marketing gimmick if I've ever heard one."

She laughed. "You're right. But I like the color."

At least she wasn't too upset about him ransacking her bag, he thought, and absently wiped his greasy fingers on his shirt.

"Oh, no," she said, dismayed, looking at his chest. "I can't believe you just did that."

Mason looked down. There was a broad orangey-red smear across the white fabric.

"Damn it," he snapped.

"You might want to get that dry-cleaned. It won't come out in the regular laundry."

She dug in her bag for a paper napkin and handed it to him, and Mason wiped the rest of the lipstick off his fingers.

"It's inevitable when I wear white. The only question when I put on this shirt was, what will I spill on myself today?"

"You can tell people it's an avant-garde screen print," Emily said. "Another game?"

Mason would have been happy to quit now, but he got to his feet and said, "Let's do it."

She beat him again, but at least he managed to make a few points, pushing it to a deuce. Gathering up their bags, they walked back to her office together, and stopped outside the entrance.

"Let me know if you have any follow-up questions about the project," Emily said. "Jen can put you in touch with other volunteers."

"Apologies again for messing up your lipstick."

"I feel bad that it wound up on your shirt," she said, eyeing the orangey smudge.

Mason glanced down at it again as he walked to his bike. It looked like he'd been stabbed. Why hadn't he thought to bring a change of clothes? He didn't even have a clean shirt in his office.

Right now that careless omission felt like professional negligence.

Cycling to the metro, he could feel the muscles he'd used for tennis, not protesting yet but telling him they were aware they'd been worked. Thinking through the events of the morning, he just couldn't believe that Emily was trying to steal from Rovski, or sabotage him. She was so straightforward, and easy to be around. He knew that skilled manipulators often came across as amiable, but she seemed guileless, and so did Stella. But that was the wrong attitude. He was supposed to be figuring out what she was up to, and today he hadn't even broached the subject. Even worse, he couldn't see a clear path to get to that point.

TWELVE

ONCE HE WAS DOWNTOWN, he ascended out of the station and cycled to the central library, locking up his bicycle outside. His stomach was rumbling after all that racket-swinging and dodging and diving, and he went into the coffee place in the lobby.

When the barista came to the register, he ordered an espresso and asked her, "Are any of these muffins vegan?"

"Nope," she said, not meeting his gaze, and started the espresso machine.

Mason grabbed a packet of almonds and an apple from the display and pulled out his wad of cash.

As she handed him his change, she eyed his shirt. "You should wear one of those bib napkins when you have ribs for lunch."

"It's lipstick," he said flatly.

"Really? With your coloring, you should wear something more on the pink side of the palette."

"Thank you," Mason said, scowling at her as he stuffed the bills in the pocket of his shorts and gathered up his purchases. "That's very helpful."

The place wasn't busy, and he sat at a table over by the window for a minute to eat his fruit and nuts and savor the coffee. Glancing at his phone, he saw that there was a text from Rovski:

Any developments?

A twinge of guilt struck, and he took a moment to formulate a reply:

Spent the morning with our target. Doing some research today. More tomorrow.

No way was Rovski going to pay him for nothing, and right now that's all he had. He pushed himself out of the chair, feeling several muscles that didn't usually get a workout protest the effort, and went into the library's atrium, riding the escalator down to the floor with all the metaphysical books. He got set up at a desk near the stacks and pulled out his computer.

The only tangible connection between Stella and Emily was that jagged astrological symbol. Astrology was so ubiquitous, he knew, that the noise online would drown out anything of value. What he needed was the curated content of books. Just to be sure, though, he searched the Web for "Aquarius symbol." The millions of results that came up were headed by "Six Foods Aquarians Should Never Eat," "Grow Your Stock Portfolio the Aquarian Way," and "How to Tell If Your Aquarian Boyfriend Is a Cheating Dirtbag." After scanning a few pages, he gave up and opened the library catalog.

Searching for books on the history of Western astrology brought up a whole section, and rather than reading the catalog he went to the shelf where they were housed and flipped through the volumes. A couple of them looked promising, and he took them back to his desk to dig through the content. It was interesting stuff, some of it paralleling the classical mythology he'd been reading, but nothing jumped out at him as meaningful, and nothing evoked Stella or Emily or the interactions he'd had with them.

Eventually he sat back and rubbed his eyes, debating whether to go through more books or call it a day. The answer came with the buzz of his phone in his shorts. It was a text from Ned:

At work? Driving past your building in a few minutes if you want a ride. I have the Crown Vic.

His thumb-typed a succinct reply:

At the library. Meet you out front.

Sliding his computer in beside the tennis racket, he made his way up to the street and saw that dusk had already descended. It was overcast again, the clouds lit by the city lights, and without a jacket he shivered in the cool air as he unlocked his bicycle and wheeled it to the curb. Something different from last week's atmospheric river was happening now, as the clouds were lower, and they weren't moving, and the air smelled damp, with the tang of ozone building up.

Mason had his front wheel off by the time the Crown Vic pulled up and rolled to a stop. Ned got out to help load the bike into the trunk, eyeing Mason's shirt.

"Is that taco sauce?"

"It's lipstick."

Ned chuckled. "Wait till I'm sitting down to tell me how that happened."

Climbing in the passenger side, Mason sank into the comfortable seat and dropped his head on the headrest.

"Do you want to eat at that place on Sunset?" Ned said, eyeing the mirror and pulling away from the curb.

"I'm not really dressed for an evening out. I'll feel like an idiot wearing shorts."

"A good percentage of the people floating around this town are dressed weirder than you."

"Good point," Mason said. "I suppose the more significant fact is that no one but me cares what I look like."

"So how did you get lipstick on your shirt?"

Mason told the story as Ned negotiated the traffic on the surface streets heading out of downtown. When they crossed under the 101 and into a hilly neighborhood, the clouds seemed to be just above the car.

"They said there might be fog tonight," Ned said, pulling into a street space near the restaurant.

Inside it was busy and boisterous and loud, but the host found them a table. As the waitress approached, she eyed Mason's shirt.

"Is that blood?" she said, her brow furrowing. "Sir, this is a vegan restaurant."

Ned chuckled and said, "Busted."

Mason sighed. "The only thing I killed today was a tube of lipstick."

"You're supposed to put it on your lips," she said.

"I'll keep that in mind."

"Do you need a cocktail?"

"Probably, but I'm not going to order one," Mason said. "Bring me the posole."

She nodded, writing it down. Ned ordered a pizza, and she stepped away.

"Why were you downtown?" Mason said.

"I was driving through. I had to pick up some stuff I ordered in the wholesale food district."

"They couldn't ship it to you?"

"I was lucky they were even willing to import it for me. It's a batch of *recado*—a spice mix from Yucatán. It's as close as you can get to Mayan cooking."

"I'll look forward to it."

"If you don't mind, I'll drop Gilbert's share of it on the way home. The minimum quantity that they let me order was huge, so I split it into three."

Mason frowned. "Gilbert doesn't cook. I'd be shocked if he has anything besides beer in his fridge."

"When I was telling him about how amazing this *recado* was going to be, he decided he wanted some. It's to impress a woman."

"Gilbert's dating someone? He didn't talk about her when he was over for dinner."

"I think she's new."

"Please tell me it's not one of the ESL tourists he accosted at that metro station."

Ned chuckled. "She's local, and Latin. Thus the desire for the *recado*."

Mason had eaten only fruit and almonds

today, and the hearty soup was satisfying. When the waitress brought the check, Ned handed her a card, and soon they were outside on the street. The fog had settled in, making the headlights of the cars cruising past on Sunset look gray and blurry. It wasn't too dense here, but once they had driven into the hills, heading to Gilbert's neighborhood, it got thicker.

"Looks like we're getting socked in," Ned muttered.

He pulled the Crown Vic in behind Gilbert's absurdly oversize SUV, the only indication that anyone was here, and killed the engine. The house, higher up the driveway, in the darkness beyond the reach of the streetlights, was just a shadowy, eerie hulking shape in the fog. No one lived in the ground-floor apartment, sensibly, at the order of the county officials who'd yellow-tagged the structure. Upstairs Gilbert had covered all the windows with metal foil, to keep the radio waves out, he said. It probably wasn't as effective as the mesh on the windows of the Bunker, as that had been put up by scientists who knew what they were doing. In Gilbert's case, blotting out the light also served to ward off unwanted attention. The downside was that his apartment felt like it was underground, even in broad daylight. He'd put his kitchen table and chairs up on the flat roof above so that he could at least get occasional exposure to the sun.

Ned reached into the backseat and grabbed a paper bag.

"This is the *recado*," he said, and handed it to Mason.

Holding it to his nose, he didn't even have to open the bag to detect the peppers, and garlic, and other heady ingredients.

"It smells amazing."

Ned took it back, and they both climbed out, carefully walking up the driveway in the darkness and the swirling fog. The stairs at the side of the house weren't visible until they were practically on top of them.

"Over here," Ned said, and Mason heard him step onto the metal stair.

"I can't believe he does this every day," Mason said, following him up.

"I suppose you'd get used to it."

"Like being blind," Mason muttered.

On Gilbert's landing, Ned banged on the heavy steel door with the heel of his fist. A moment later it swung open. Even though the light inside was dim, it made Mason wince after navigating the dark driveway. Gilbert beckoned them inside and kissed them both.

"Do you want something to drink?"

"We can't stay," Ned said, and handed him the bag.

Gilbert held it to his nose and inhaled. "Oh, man, that's the stuff."

"You have to read up on it before you cook with it," Ned said. "A little goes a long way."

Gilbert tossed the bag onto the sofa behind him, then looked pointedly at Mason's shirt. "Spaghetti for lunch?"

"Something like that."

"I feel a little guilty that I was so hard on you the other day," Gilbert said.

"I know that it comes from a place of concern. Have you been reading about addiction?"

"Did Ned tell you that?"

"I intuited it psychically," Mason said.

Gilbert frowned, dubious, and stepped over to the coffee table to retrieve a book, handing it to him. The title was *Class, Race and Tequila Shots: Digging Deeper into Addiction*. Mason scanned the description on the back cover.

"It looks intense."

"We all need to wake up," Gilbert said. "I just hope that you'll choose to use your white privilege for a higher purpose."

Mason handed the book back, frowning as he repressed an angry retort. "I'll get right on that, Hombre."

There was no spark of recognition in Gilbert's eyes. "You've never called me that before."

"It's not really the best nickname for him,"

Ned said.

"Why not?" Mason said, raising his eyebrows.

"Let's just call him Gilbert."

"You call each other '*cabrón*.'"

"Maybe the rule is that you can only call people nicknames in a language that you actually speak," Ned said.

Mason chuckled. "Fair enough."

Saying good-bye to Gilbert elicited another tight hug and a neck kiss for each of them, and once his door was closed, they felt their way down the stairs to the driveway in the misty blackness.

"I have one more stop," Ned said, as they climbed into the Crown Vic. "The other person who came in on the order lives near here. Her name is Cat."

"Fine with me," Mason said. "Although it's hard to believe that in a city of five million Latinos, you can't just buy *recado* at the market."

"You can, but not this *recado*," he said, craning to peer out the rear window as he backed into the street.

"Who's Cat? I've never heard you talk about her."

"I only know her from work. She deals with the Latin American banks. Her name is actually Catalina, but everyone calls her Cat."

Ned drove through the hilly neighborhood, deftly maneuvering the big old car on the narrow streets. The fog seemed to be getting thicker. Reclining on the headrest, Mason watched the billowing haze and the fuzzy headlights of oncoming vehicles as they went past. Eventually Ned made a left and pulled to the curb. The narrow street had an uphill grade, and Mason heard the clicking of the parking brake as Ned pressed it down with his foot.

"Do you want to meet Cat?" he asked, reaching into the backseat for another paper bag.

"I don't think I have the energy. Plus I look like a sporty ax murderer."

Ned chuckled. "I won't be long."

Mason cracked the window and shifted down in the seat, getting more comfortable, watching the slowly drifting fog. It was obscuring the houses up the block now, the streetlamps above just nebulous white blotches in the clouds. The street was quiet, with no passing traffic, and he heard a man's voice calling something in the distance.

The tone of his voice rose and fell, like a chant, like he was trying to summon his dog, or his kid. The second time was louder, and Mason could make out the words. "Chron ... icle." It took him a second to put it together. Not two words, just one: *Chronicle*. Nobody would name their kid that, or even their dog. He was hawking a newspaper.

The second time, the voice was louder. "Chron … icle." In the side mirror, Mason watched as the man stepped out of the swirling fog, strolling up the sidewalk. As he passed the car, he saw that the guy was wearing retro tweed golf pants and a floppy cap, a bulky canvas bag slung over one shoulder. Mason had to grin. The guy was dedicated to his job, dressing up old-school like that.

It was a little odd that he was headed up the hill. The boulevard and its better sales opportunities were in the opposite direction. Up there were only houses and maybe some apartments. And why was he hawking newspapers at night? The man had disappeared into the fog, but Mason heard him again, farther away. "Chron … icle."

Thinking about it, there was no paper in town called *Chronicle*. And there were definitely no newsboys anymore. Either Mason had completely lost his grip on reality, or he'd shifted into another state of mind. This had to be a dream, he decided. That meant he needed to navigate it consciously.

"Be here now," he murmured to himself, and unbuckled his seat belt.

As he looked down, he saw that he was wearing his gray 1950s suit, not the soiled tennis shirt. Pulling on the door handle, he stepped out onto the sidewalk, and walked up the hill, the same way the newsboy had gone. The fog was so dense now that he could only see a few feet ahead.

"Herman," Mason called, resisting the temptation to chant it like the newsboy, splitting the syllables, with the rising and falling tone.

In a few more paces, Herman appeared out of the fog, walking toward him, a smile on his face.

"Lo, the wandering psychic. You're looking spiffy."

"It's vintage," Mason said, self-consciously adjusting the knot of his necktie.

Herman looked the way he always had, in a dark shirt with red suspenders and that flat worker's cap. Tonight he didn't have his violin with him.

"You're not busking?" Mason said.

"Now and then I am," he said casually, and tossed something to him underhand, adding, "Catch."

Mason managed to snag it out of the air. It was a tangerine, in that beautiful oranger-than-orange color. He admired it for a moment, then pulled it apart, leaning over to spare his suit and biting into the segments. It was lush and delicious.

"We should go to the stadium," Herman said.

"Give me a second here," Mason said, still engrossed in eating. Once he was finished, he looked at Herman. "What stadium?"

"You'll see," he said, and looped his arm through Mason's.

They took a step farther up the sidewalk and were no longer in the fog, instead inside a broad tunnel, gently sloping upward toward a brightly lit rectangle outside at the end. A sea of stadium bleachers rose in the distance. Herman let go of his arm. As they walked toward the opening, they passed several people going the other way. None of them were in sports uniforms, despite the venue, and none of them made eye contact, or showed any interest in them.

Stepping out of the tunnel, they were on the grassy field, marked with white lines and stretching to the distant stands. There were other people here too, walking around, a few dotting the tiers of bleachers. Herman continued onto the field. The space was vast when you were in the middle of it, Mason realized. The stands were all around, forming the horizon, and the wide black sky yawned overhead, but the bright stadium lights blotted out the stars.

Pondering the space, Mason wondered if the game was about to begin. The few people that were here looked like spectators, not players, but those big lights wouldn't be turned on unless something was about to happen. Whatever game it was, soon all eyes would be focused on the ball. When he'd been playing tennis today, in the relatively narrow confines of the court, it was easy to keep track of the little chartreuse sphere in its arc. But here, in this vast space, any ball would become a tiny speck.

The grass below, and the dome of the sky. It was reminiscent of where he'd stretched out on the canvas with Stella. What was he doing here? He resisted the urge to ask Herman, who was gazing up at the stands. This realm wasn't supposed to be about the linear pursuit of tangible goals.

Someone was walking toward them, and Mason turned to look. The big nose, the shaggy hair—it was Hombre.

"How can you be here?" Mason demanded. "I just saw you, and you were wide awake."

Hombre just grinned. "Remember what the manicurist said."

"Did she send you? That would be really annoying, if she asked you to come and coach me."

He waved impatiently. "What did she say?"

Mason thought about that. Hanh said lots of stuff, but he worked to sort out specifically what was relevant to right now.

"Time and distance are less important here," he said finally.

Hombre nodded. "Right. They don't really matter."

"So?" he said, throwing up his hands.

"So you just answered your own question. You know what you're doing here."

Maybe he did, Mason thought. Maybe it was already in his head, like muscle memory. Focusing on his thoughts for a moment, he imagined stepping sideways, shifting his consciousness, willing himself to go deeper. Insight came as his mind made the shift.

He turned to Herman. "I want to show you something."

It took Herman a second to pull his attention away from the stadium. His eyes were bright, and he had a wry smile on his face. "Don't you want to watch the game? I think they're about to get started."

"We'd be in the way, standing here," Mason said.

"You're not really dressed for it either," Hombre said, giving Mason's suit the once-over.

Ignoring him, Mason took Herman's arm and thought about how Stella had found the way across the lake, following an invisible line. This time he was the one who had to navigate. There was a route-finding technique that he'd learned. Focusing his thoughts on the surface of the field, he tried to intuit the lines that he knew were just below the grass. It was easier than in waking life, and in this deeper state of mind he realized that he could find the way.

"Let's go," he said, and with a single step the stadium was gone. They were in the grassy meadow where he and Stella had landed, the canvas sheet still stretched out in the moonlight. She wasn't here, he saw, looking around, and Hombre hadn't come with them either.

Herman slowly walked around the perimeter of the canvas, gazing at it.

"Does this mean anything to you?" Mason said, watching him.

He didn't answer, but stopped and squatted beside the sheet. "Help me lift this," he called.

Mason went over to see what he was talking about. A flat rock was partly buried at the edge of the grass. Herman dropped to his knees, exploring the underside with his fingers.

Mason hesitated, leery of getting grass stains on his suit, but then knelt beside him. "This is rattlesnake country. Did you know that rattlesnakes hang out under rocks?"

"Not this rock," Herman said, and grasped it, gesturing with his chin.

Taking hold of the end, Mason positioned his fingers beside Herman's, and they heaved on it together, but barely managed to budge it.

"Again," Herman said.

Straining to lift the rock, they slowly pulled it free of the earth. Mason tumbled back on his butt as it came loose, and Herman tugged at the rock with both hands, flipping it over. There was an open space below it, and before Mason could admonish him again about snakes, Herman thrust his hand in and pulled out a pair of boots. Mason watched in amazement as he brushed the dirt off them. They were made of brown canvas, with high tops and dull yellow laces.

"I needed something like these," Herman said. "My feet get sore when I'm busking."

"It's more than busking, though, right? It's your vocation."

Herman eyed him. "I don't know about that. But these will be helpful."

Mason snapped awake when Ned pulled open the driver's door, and he squinted as the dome light suddenly illuminated the interior of the Crown Vic. Herman and the meadow were gone.

"You look sleepy," Ned said, twisting the key in the ignition.

"I drifted off," Mason mumbled. "Tennis took a lot out of me."

On the way home, they rode in comfortable silence as Ned maneuvered the car down to the boulevard. The visibility was still murky, although once they were out of the hills, Mason could see for a block or more.

The experience in the fog felt more vivid than any dream, and more permanent. Hombre had been there to help him, to shift his thoughts, or maybe to jog his memory. That guy had helped him a couple of times now, he realized, had pointed him in the right direction. It seemed ludicrous that Gilbert was so much more competent in that world than here. Whatever he was picking up from his alien abductions must be beneficial. Gilbert wasn't calling them abductions anymore, he remembered, because he said he participated willingly. In any case, Mason was going to have to work out a way not to be resentful of him.

The fog was heavier again in their neighborhood, and Ned pulled all the way to the side to let an oncoming car descend their hilly street. A few minutes later he made it into the garage.

"We don't see that kind of fog very often," Mason said, looping his arm through Ned's as they walked to the house.

"I'm glad we weren't on the freeway. It's supposed to burn off in the morning."

As they stepped in, the lights were down low. One of the lounge chairs, facing the French doors, slowly rotated to reveal Peggy, dressed in jeans and a sweater, sitting there with a tumbler in her hand.

"Is that scotch?" Ned said, closing the door behind them.

"It seemed appropriate for watching the fog roll in," she said.

"You ruined it with the ice."

She scoffed and eyed Mason's shirt. "Bird strike while you were cycling?"

"Finally, I can take this damn thing off." He set down his backpack and then pulled the shirt over his head and went into the kitchen.

"Whoa," Peggy said. "Too much melanin-deficient flesh. I'm going to go snow-blind."

"As Peggy is my witness," Mason said, dropping his shirt in the trash, "I shall never wear white again."

"Never is a long time, Scarlett," Peggy said.

Watching him wash his hands in the kitchen sink, Ned said, "We could probably get the lipstick out of it."

"It doesn't matter. I'm not wearing it again. It's a wrong shirt."

"Lipstick?" Peggy asked, the ice in her tumbler tinkling as she swirled it.

"It's a long story."

"Mason's well-known whirl of perpetual confusion," Ned said.

Mason shot him a look. "It's only confusing if you don't get what's going on."

"Pour yourself a scotch and sit a spell," Peggy said. "You can tell me about it."

"Let me get a shirt," Mason said, and went down the hall.

When he came back, Ned was in the kitchen.

"Would you two hate me if I stink up the place with *recado*?" he said. "I want to try it on this fresh corn."

"Not if we get to eat it," Peggy said.

Mason sprawled on the sofa and told her about his case, and playing tennis, and mangling Emily's lipstick, which elicited a laugh.

"You're lucky she was so understanding," Peggy said. "Makeup is expensive."

Ned brought them little bowls of spicy corn, cut fresh off the cob, and the three of them talked about the ingredients in the *recado*. Even though he was physically tired, Mason lingered, enjoying the conversation.

THIRTEEN

IN THE MORNING HE had no memory of dreaming, and came to wakefulness gradually, not harangued by an alarm, lying in bed, enjoying the daylight streaming in the windows. He was missing something, he knew—it was slightly beyond reach, just outside his awareness, and he couldn't quite get to it.

The simplest psychic technique was to clear his mind and wait for it to drift in, so he closed his eyes and worked to do that. Usually that induced the objective state Matt had described, but he wasn't yet fully awake, so it was hard to focus on anything, and random images flitted through his awareness. The sailcloth, spread out on the ground, he remembered. Herman finding those boots, and hanging out on the canvas with Stella. *Take that up with Lorenzo,* Emily had said, walking into that lab in the Bunker. Mason opened his eyes, gazing at the bright sky outside the window. Why had he forgotten about that until now?

Rolling out of bed, he got dressed and went to the kitchen. Ned was gone, probably to see his parents for lunch after his mom came home from mass. Peggy was out too, leaving the house empty and quiet. Mason took his computer to the kitchen counter, and made a pot of espresso before he sat down and got to work.

Peering at the screen, he searched for "Lorenzo" and "Phaethon." The first result in the list was a company called Sail Folding LLC. It was just a business listing, without a website, showing that someone named Lorenzo Vargas was the registered owner. Why it came up in connection to Phaethon wasn't clear, but the company's address was on Tangerine Court in Rio Bosque. That couldn't be a coincidence—he'd been seeing tangerines, eating them even, in his waking life and in his sleep. Checking the map, he found that Tangerine Court was near Rayborn College, in the neighborhood where Emily had eluded him on her bike. A smile spread across his face. This had to be connected to her.

After he hurriedly ate one of yesterday's give-away tangerines and some other fruit, he checked the weather. Ned was right—the fog had burned off everywhere, and it was warming up, finally, after weeks of winter cold. Not bothering with a jacket, he pulled on his backpack, then coasted down the hill to the metro.

When he got to the commercial neighborhood in Rio Bosque, cycling the empty streets, it felt dead quiet. He hadn't thought of that—it was Sunday, so nobody was working. Still, this was the neighborhood where he'd followed Emily. She could easily have turned onto Tangerine Court, and workday or not, he had to check out Sail Folding LLC.

When he found the right building, Mason looked around for a place to lock his bike, and rode half a block farther to a parking sign, then walked back. Inside the glass of the door was a small sign that read SAIL FOLDING in block letters, with no logo, no embellishments. It looked like a sheet of printer paper, like the PHAETHON sign taped to the lab door in the Bunker. He couldn't see inside, as the glass was frosted, but the place looked as dead as all its neighbors. There was a bell beside the entrance, so he pressed it and listened. No sound came from within, and he considered walking around the back, but then the door swung open.

The guy standing there was in his twenties, tall and with bony cheeks. With dark hair like Ned's, he looked Latin, and wore jeans and a T-shirt. On a lanyard around his neck was an ID with the logo of Rayborn College. Mason couldn't read the fine print from this distance, but he didn't have to.

The guy looked him over and frowned. "Can I help you?"

"You must be Lorenzo."

"Who are you?"

"Mason. I wanted to ask you about Phaethon."

"Where did you hear that name?" he demanded.

"I was in the Bunker. Am I not supposed to know about Phaethon?"

"We only use that name in-house. The official name is the Solar Sail Project."

"Which is what, exactly?" Mason said.

"Dude—who are you?"

"A friend of Emily's."

His face clouded, and he stepped back inside, pulling the door wide. Mason saw that it was a small front office, with a couple of desks and little else—no art on the walls, no plants, no cabinets. The thin carpet bore the boxy impressions of furniture that had once stood on it. It looked like someone was just about to vacate.

Lorenzo turned to the inner door and shouted, "Emily."

Mason stepped inside. Pushing through the door from the back, Emily walked in, a look of annoyance on her face. Today she was dressed for manual labor, like Lorenzo, in jeans and a sweatshirt.

"Why are you shouting?" she demanded, and then caught sight of Mason. Her expression shifted, her eyes growing wide. "What are you doing here?"

"Research," Mason said flatly.

"He's asking about Phaethon," Lorenzo said.

"I thought you were writing about fruit."

"I'm more interested in Phaethon, and the solar energy sail."

"Not solar energy," Lorenzo said, furrowing his brow. "It's the Solar Sail Project."

Mason nodded. "Exactly what I meant."

"What's going on?" she said. "What do you know about Phaethon?"

"Nothing," he said, spreading his hands. "I'd love to hear all about it."

"He's working for a competitor," Lorenzo said.

"I doubt it," Emily said, still eyeing Mason. "We don't really have any of those."

"Is this some kind of scam?" Lorenzo said, raising his voice.

"I don't think it is." Emily's demeanor was calm. "The press releases are going out tonight anyway. It'll all be public soon."

"What will?" Mason said, raising his eyebrows.

"Don't tell him anything," Lorenzo said. "We don't know him. We don't know what he's up to."

Mason ignored him, holding Emily's gaze. "A press release—that sounds enlightening. Maybe I could get a copy of that."

"No way," Lorenzo said. "It's embargoed until launch time."

Turning to Lorenzo, Emily said, "Don't be so suspicious. Mason is a journalist. I assume he wants to write about us." She looked back to Mason. "It explains why you asked me about my side business the other day. Where did you hear about Phaethon?"

"I saw the name taped to a door in building 42."

"That's the assembly lab," she said. "How did you know I was connected to Phaethon?"

"I saw you walk in there."

Emily watched him for a moment before she turned back to Lorenzo. "It can't hurt to answer some of his questions. It's basically free publicity."

Lorenzo folded his arms and scowled, but he held his tongue.

"Sit down, if you want," Emily said, and perched on the edge of one of the desks.

Mason pulled out the desk chair and set his backpack between his feet, watching as Lorenzo positioned himself in front of the door into the back room.

"It looks like you're clearing out of here," Mason said, glancing around the barren office.

"Soon," Emily said. "We don't need the space anymore."

"What were you using it for? And what were you doing in the Bunker?"

"I thought you knew about the project."

"Tell me your version of it," Mason said. "Imagine that I don't know anything at all."

Lorenzo scoffed, and Emily turned to glare at him before she spoke.

"We're using our skills in mathematics to design a way to fold up a solar sail to fly on the spacecraft. We called the sail Phaethon, although officially it doesn't have a name. It's just 'the sail.' I handle the more theoretical aspects, and Lorenzo does the coding to run computer simulations."

"So you're both academics, and you're working for Sail Folding LLC on the side."

"We're not working for the LLC. The LLC is the two of us. We set it up specifically for this project."

"You're doing this for the government?" Mason said.

"It's a private spacecraft. We're subcontracting for another company."

"What's a solar sail?"

Emily frowned and shifted position. "If you don't know anything about it, how did you find this place?"

"When you set up a company, that information is in the public domain," Mason said. That wasn't the whole truth, and before she could formulate a follow-up, he added, "I'm just trying to be thorough here. I don't want to make any assumptions, and I want to be sure I understand it all."

"A solar sail is like the sail on a ship," she said, "but instead of catching wind for propulsion, it catches particles from the sun—the solar wind."

"Why does it take two mathematicians and a workshop to get it folded up?"

"Phaethon is a complex object. It's huge—almost twelve meters in diameter. It's round but not flat, with slight concave curvature to the surface when it's deployed. It has to be extremely compact and durable to go into space. Mathematics is how we designed the optimal way to fold it up so that it won't get damaged in transit, and so that it won't snarl when it unfurls."

"What is it made of?"

"A very thin, very strong plastic with a mirrored surface. Someone else created the material. We're just folding it."

"I see," Mason said, absorbing it all. "So why does a spaceship need a sail?"

"It'll never run out of propellant," Emily said. "Think of a sailboat. It doesn't need gasoline, so it can keep going as long as there's wind. The solar wind is constant and inexhaustible."

Mason nodded. "What did you mean that the press releases were going out tonight?"

"The launch is this evening from Vandenberg. We're driving up there to watch. The spacecraft reaches orbit about ten minutes after liftoff, and Phaethon will deploy a few hours later. It will carry the craft to L2 to do research." She waved her hand and added, "L2 means Lagrange point 2."

He decided not to ask what that meant. "Phaethon is what you call the sail, but what's the name of the spaceship?"

"It's known by an acronym: *L2SPRV*. I'll put you on the press release distribution list. It won't go out until after the actual launch."

"Is that a security precaution?"

"Vandenberg is a military base—they've got plenty of security. The press release is embargoed because launches are often delayed for technical reasons. We don't want to brag about something ahead of time, and get a bunch of attention, and then have it look like we bungled it."

"So you've already figured out how to fold up the sail."

Lorenzo smirked. "It sounds so trivial when

you put it like that. But yes, our work on this project is finished."

"I know that rigging sails is complicated," Mason said. "Is this the first time you're doing it?"

"The first of many," Emily said.

"If it actually works," Mason said.

"It's going to work," Lorenzo said, and frowned. "All the simulations show our design to be foolproof."

Mason eyed him. "I wonder if the people who designed the *Titanic* used that word, or the people who built all those nuclear reactors that blew up and melted into the earth? Or has someone solved an equation that eliminated scientific hubris?"

"You know nothing about this," Emily said firmly. "You should stick to writing about fruit."

Mason met her gaze. "Why did you need to use Rovski's bank statement?"

Emily recoiled. "Is that what this is about? You sneaky little devil."

"So you're not denying it."

"How did you know about that?"

"First, tell me what you were trying to do."

"There's nothing sinister in it, Mason. I didn't think Rovski would mind."

"You mean you didn't think he knew," Mason said, furrowing his brow. "Of course he minds. You're stealing from him."

Lorenzo stood up straighter, concern clouding his expression.

"I didn't steal anything," Emily said, raising her voice.

Mason threw up his hands. "So what were you doing?"

Emily pressed her mouth into a hard line, eyeing him. He could see the wheels turning as she calculated what she was going to say.

"He's bluffing," Lorenzo said. "He doesn't know what he's talking about."

Mason ignored him and watched Emily. "Just tell me the truth. You shouldn't have to think about it."

Finally she spoke. "We needed to show some hard assets to get credit from our bankers. We were scrambling with unexpected expenses during our work on Phaethon."

"You paid for the whole spaceship, or just the sail?"

Lorenzo scoffed. "Are you kidding me? This is a huge project. Phaethon is just one small part of it. We didn't pay for any of the hardware."

"Do you know what happened to the guy named Phaethon in the Greek tale?" Mason demanded, glaring at him. "He hijacked the sun and set the planet on fire, so the gods intervened and blew him out of the sky."

"I know all that now," Lorenzo said. "I didn't

when we picked that name."

"That's why it's not the official name," Emily said.

"Sometimes you have to read to the end of the story," Mason said, louder than he'd planned. He looked to Emily. "If you didn't finance the stupid space scow, what did you need credit for?"

"We had to pay for test materials to make sure our folding schema would work. It functioned beautifully in computer simulation, but we needed to test the durability and compression of real materials."

"If it doesn't work in space, do you still get paid?"

"We've already been paid," she said, "but not enough. When the sail works as planned, we'll get other contracts that will more than cover our debts."

"Why do you need this place?" Mason said, waving his arm at the room. "Why not work in building 42?"

"That's where they assembled the spacecraft. We need our own workshop for development."

Mason sighed. "So you weren't planning to drain Rovski's bank accounts."

"Nothing like that. We were just using him as a straw investor."

"We're not crooks," Lorenzo said.

"I'm pretty sure what you did qualifies as

fraud," Mason said. "Did you impersonate Rovski in meetings, or just on paper? You must have forged his signature at some point."

"Are you going to make trouble for us?" Emily said.

"I don't care about your origami space sail," Mason said, gesturing dismissively. "Whether this is trouble for you or not is up to Rovski. You have to talk to the guy. He's totally freaked out. He thinks you're trying to mess with him."

"I didn't know that he knew."

"You got him locked out of his accounts at the college. He knows it was you."

"Oh, god." She winced and put her hand on the back of her neck. "I needed documentation about his job, and his salary. I didn't change anything, or take anything. It was all just to get credit."

"You were supposed to handle Rovski," Lorenzo said.

Emily waved a hand, not looking at him. "I'll talk to him in the next day or two. It's going to be hectic tomorrow with the spacecraft's maneuvers."

"It's not just about handling him," Mason said. "Rovski hasn't gone to the cops yet because he thinks you're at the center of a conspiracy to ruin his life. You have to come clean, and you have to apologize. He's a reasonable guy. If you clear the air, maybe he won't turn you in."

"What are you going to do?" Lorenzo said, jutting his chin at Mason.

"That's up to Rovski. If you work it out with him, I'll step away."

Lorenzo didn't look convinced, but Emily nodded, relief in her eyes.

"Deal," she said.

Mason stood up and pulled on his backpack.

"Do you trust him with this?" Lorenzo said, taking a step toward Mason. "He could burn us to the ground."

Mason put his hands on his hips. "You don't have any other options, chum—unless you plan on trying to detain me right now, or worse. That would take things to a whole other level. Kidnapping will land you twenty years of eating baloney sandwiches in San Quentin. You'd be better off copping to the fraud."

"You ginger freak," Lorenzo spat.

"Calm down, both of you," Emily snapped, her tone sharp, holding her index finger in the air. They both looked at her, and more calmly, she said to Lorenzo, "I'm inclined to take the man at his word. We have a rapport." She looked to Mason. "To clarify, are you really a journalist, or just a friend of Rovski's?"

"I'm a psychic investigator."

"Seriously?" Lorenzo broke into a broad smile. "At least we know that he's not a threat. Nobody is going to believe anything he says."

Emily scowled. "Rovski hired a psychic? That guy is such a weirdo. And how did you connect me to Phaethon, and to this company? My name's not listed on the business license."

"His Ouija board told him," Lorenzo said.

"I'm not going to bother explaining it," Mason said. "You wouldn't believe me."

"You're right," Lorenzo said. "I certainly wouldn't believe it, because psychic power is bullshit."

Emily glared at him. "Just shut up for a minute." Turning to Mason, she said, "You can't just leave it like that. You have to tell me."

Mason closed his eyes for a second and took a breath. "The truth, as I understand it: you and I went sailing, on a little daysailer on a lake, and you showed me Phaethon, or at least a representation of it, spread out on the grass. That's part of why we trust each other, I think—a minute ago you said you felt it too, when you used the word *rapport*. We played tennis, but we also went sailing, and talked about the stars."

"You were in some kind of trance?" Emily said.

"You were too. I met another version of you— from your subconscious mind."

Lorenzo couldn't contain himself. "Ha!" he cackled, and held out his palms, then lowered his voice, mimicking Mason's. "It was all a dream."

"I didn't dream up you forging Rovski's bank statement, and breaking into his accounts, and impersonating him," Mason said, eyeing Lorenzo. "I've got hard evidence of that. Personally I'd call it identity theft, but a prosecutor might have other names for it."

"We've already been through that," Emily said. "I'll fix things with Rovski. I gave you my word."

"That's good enough for now. I'm going to hang on to the documentation until Rovski's satisfied." He looked at Lorenzo. "Good luck with your plastic space trash."

Mason walked out and headed up the block to his bicycle. Lorenzo was a dick, but he knew Emily would keep her word. The rest was up to Rovski. His steps felt lighter, and he couldn't help but smile. It was a victory—he'd figured it out.

FOURTEEN

Once he got home, breathing hard from the ride up the hill, Mason found the house still quiet and empty. He sprawled on the sofa and pulled open his computer to do some research on the rocket launches from Vandenberg. There was a whole community of rocket watchers spread all over Southern California, and he spent some time perusing their website and reading the postings.

The launch times were published a few days or weeks ahead, they explained, although the listing that the military provided didn't always include details of what they were putting into space, which led to much speculation about spy satellites. The launch time was given as a range of a few minutes to a few hours, and the hobbyists said that a launch usually happened in the first second of that window. If it didn't, it was probably going to be delayed by a day or more. Most of the launches were in the early morning, with the darkness providing good viewing conditions. Daytime launches weren't visible unless you were close to the base in Santa Barbara County.

Launches were most visible when they happened after sunset, when the sky was dark but the rocket exhaust was high enough to be lit by the sun from below the horizon. Those tended to freak people out, it seemed, especially in the metropolis, when weird lights and huge glowing contrails were visible in the sky at a time of day when lots of people were outside.

Mason checked the list of upcoming launches, and as Emily had promised, there was one today, scheduled for a window of 19:02 to 20:46. It took a minute to figure out what time that corresponded to. Next he looked up when sunset was. It would get dark just before the launch. That meant it would be visible from the city. When he checked the weather, the forecasters were confident that the skies were going to remain clear tonight.

Folding his computer closed, he went to the kitchen and looked in the fridge, where he found a container of Ned's leftover chili, and ate a few forkfuls as he formulated a plan. There wasn't much left, so he ate it all, then put the empty container in the dishwasher and went back to the sofa, where he pulled out his phone. He was glad that Rovski picked up.

"I have some answers for you," Mason said. "Can you come by my office this evening?"

"Did you find out what Emily is up to?"

"I did. I'll give you a full report. Can you be there at six?"

"You want me to meet you in person," Rovski said, "so that I'll be sure to pay you."

"That's not the only reason, but it's a good idea. Definitely bring the dough."

"So it's five hundred times three days."

"Five days," Mason said. "I worked on this today."

"But we stopped the clock on Friday. So that makes four days."

"You came to my office in a panic on Friday. That restarted the clock."

"Can we say four and a half days?" Rovski said.

Such a cheapskate, Mason thought. He'd worked on this day and night—literally when he was asleep. "Maybe I'll provide four and a half parts out of five of the information I've uncovered," he said. "What does that work out to, like, ninety percent?"

"All right," Rovski said flatly. "I'll pay for the five days. Can I bring a check?"

"That works. And it's important that you're not late."

•••••••

A WHILE LATER NED came in, and Mason, still on the sofa, looked up from his computer.

"How was mass?"

"You're funny. If I ever darken the door of a church again, I'll probably burst into flames."

"That would be a startlingly religious experience for a nontheist to have," Mason said.

Ned chuckled and hefted the shopping bag he was carrying. "Mom sent you some tamales."

"I love that woman. Did she put my name on them?"

"No," he said flatly, and stepped into the kitchen, tucking the tamales into the fridge.

"It's fine—I'll find a Sharpie and do it myself later."

"You're allowed to share them," Ned said, walking back into the living room. "And you have to call her to say thanks."

"Have you ever seen a launch from Vandenberg?"

"Once. I didn't know what it was at first." Ned sat on the sofa at Mason's feet and started to massage his toes through his socks. "Gilbert was on the 10 that night, and he saw these bright twisted clouds forming in the sky. When he called me, he was so excited—I could hardly understand him. He thought it was the aliens finally revealing themselves."

"I hope he pulled over."

"I could see it from here," Ned said, nodding to the French doors. "I stood on the balcony and watched. Eventually we found out what it was."

"I'm sure Gilbert was disappointed. What time of day was it?"

"Just after sundown. Apparently those are the ones that are easiest to see."

"That's the consensus among the rocket watchers," Mason said, and told him about tonight's launch, and his plan to meet Rovski.

"If I'm invited, I can make food," Ned said. "It can be a dinner event."

"Right on." He sent Rovski a text:

> Dinner will be provided courtesy of Ned. See you
> at six o'clock.

Ned went to putter in the kitchen, making sandwiches and cutting up vegetables for a salad. When Mason went in to make himself an espresso, he admired the spread.

"This looks amazing."

"I'm a little worried we'll get cold after dark," Ned said.

"So we have to dress warm. We'll take that beach blanket."

●●●●●●

THE SUN WAS LOW in the west when they climbed into the Barracuda and drove downtown. Ned pulled into the garage under Mason's building. Normally he hated parking there, because he had to leave his key with the valet, but it was Sunday, and the building was quiet, so the valet wouldn't be moving his car around.

Ned grabbed the wicker basket of food and Mason carried the bulky beach blanket to the elevator. When they stepped onto the car, Ned punched the button for the top floor instead of the one for Mason's office.

"I'll get set up," he explained. "You can wait for Rovski in your office."

"I won't have to. Outside business hours, the front desk phones before they let anyone up."

The top floor had no hallways, just a couple of doors off the lobby into the penthouse, where the building's owners lived, and a door to the stairs that led up to the roof. Mason punched the code into the keypad on the handle, overriding the alarm that would sound if the fire-exit crash bar was pressed. He propped it open by flipping down the foot stop, and they trudged up the stairs.

"Your landlords don't mind?" Ned asked.

"I think they're in the South Pacific for the winter. Even if they were here, they wouldn't care."

They each held a side of the blanket to spread it out on the flat roof, ringed by a low wall. The view was dramatic, broken only on one side by the elevator machinery, and in the corner, the light-gathering fixture atop the glass column in the back stairwell. The western sky was unobstructed, and as predicted, completely cloudless. The pair of them stood there, taking it in, eventually interrupted by Mason's phone buzzing in his pants.

It was the guard at the desk downstairs, calling to say Rovski was here.

"Send him up," Mason said, and went back downstairs to his office, standing at the windows to admire the orange glow along the horizon.

Rovski knocked a moment later, and when Mason pulled open the door, he thrust a check at him.

"What is Emily doing?" Rovski demanded.

"I'll tell you all about it on the roof," Mason said, striding over to his desk to drop the check, not bothering to examine it. "I'm glad you're wearing a jacket."

Rovski waited for him to lock the office door, then followed him to the stairwell. "Why are we going to the roof?"

"To have dinner."

Mason trotted up the last flight ahead of him to find Ned had laid out the food. The space was lit by a single glaring floodlight beside the door to the stairs, casting harsh shadows, but at least the show in the sky was in the opposite direction.

"Oh, what a lovely feast," Rovski said, stepping onto the roof, his demeanor softening. "I'm so happy to have dinner with you."

"Let's eat," Ned said, and the three of them sat on the blanket.

"You have divine kitchen skills," Rovski said, once he'd eaten half his sandwich.

"I have a lot of fun with it."

"He's a maestro," Mason said.

"Tell me," Rovski said, gesturing to the fixture at the corner of the roof. "What is that? I can't stop staring at it."

"It's called the corona," Mason said.

A few feet tall and made of spiky, twisting dark-green glass, it really was an odd structure. Mason wasn't surprised it had caught his eye.

"I know it's not a decoration," Rovski said. "It's too small to be visible from the street. What is its function?"

"In the daytime it channels light into the stairwell underneath."

"It looks like a splash of water, frozen in time."

"I call it the melted pineapple."

"Does it also channel moonlight?" Ned asked, and gestured to the sky.

Mason twisted around and saw it, toward the east, just past its quarter phase, the way it was when Hombre had pointed it out to him.

"Waxing gibbous," he said, gazing at it.

"So you have news about Emily," Rovski said.

"Of course." Mason set his plate down and got into it, explaining her solar sail business, and her financial troubles, and why she'd altered his bank statement and accessed his accounts. Rovski listened intently, his eyes growing wide.

"So it was all to steal my identity," Rovski said.

"Technically she didn't take anything from you, so it's more like she borrowed your identity to help get credit. Emily thought you'd never find out about it."

"That's totally fraud," Ned said. "If she defaults on the loan, they're going to come after Rovski."

Mason shrugged. "That's not part of her plan, although I guess it could happen."

But Rovski wasn't focused on that. "So Phaethon is just a math problem."

"If folding things really is about math," Mason said.

"It's all math. That's her world as well as mine."

"I told her she had to explain it to you herself, and maybe apologize to you."

"Apologies are worthless," Ned said. "You need to go to the cops. What she did was wrong."

Rovski sighed. "I know I should be angry with her, but it's a big relief that she's not trying to steal from me."

"So I earned my fee," Mason said.

"It was extremely expensive, but yes, you found the truth."

Ned chuckled. "I forgot my binoculars in the car. How much time do we have?"

Mason glanced at his phone. "Twelve minutes."

"That's long enough," he said, and jumped up, hustling to the stairwell.

"Twelve minutes until what?" Rovski said.

"The spacecraft that Phaethon is attached to is going up tonight from Vandenberg. We might be able to see it."

Rovski smiled. "Such a brilliant way to make it concrete. You're going to show me the rocket." He poked at his salad before he spoke again. "Did you use your psychic powers to discover Emily's secrets?"

"In a way. I connected with her in the dream state. With you too."

"You dreamed of me?" he said, raising his eyebrows.

"I met you, or a version of you. You were playing the violin."

Rovski opened the top of the wicker basket

and pulled out a tangerine, then started to peel it. It was one of the ones Mason had taken from the college giveaway yesterday.

"I find that hard to believe," Rovski said, avoiding his gaze.

"Regardless, I did get you an explanation."

Mason watched him work, pulling the segments apart and savoring them, and thought about the tangerine in Herman's violin case. It was hard to draw a direct link, but then here was Rovski, eating it in front of him. It wasn't clear if he'd achieved Hanh's task either. It had been so nebulous, and surely there was more to it than helping Herman find a pair of boots. But that could be symbolic of a dozen different achievements. In a way it paralleled what he'd told Rovski this evening, giving him some peace of mind that he wasn't a target, just a convenient tool, a means to an end. So maybe he'd done what Hanh asked.

Ned returned, his binoculars hanging around his neck, and sat with them.

"Showtime," Ned said, and rubbed his hands together.

Mason checked his phone. "If it's going to happen, it should be right around now."

He gazed at the fading orange band across the western horizon, looking for signs of movement in the dark sky. All three of them reacted in the same moment, when the plume came into view, a white cone moving slowly across the sky. As it drifted, bright sprawling clouds expanded in its wake.

"It's just like the one I saw before," Ned said.

Rovski murmured, "It's beautiful."

"It looks like it's headed sideways, not up," Mason said.

"That's an optical illusion," Rovski said. "It's because the earth is curved. When the first Sputnik went up, the ground crew thought the same thing, that it had failed to reach orbit. But it did."

Ned offered his binoculars, but even with magnification it was impossible to see the rocket itself, only the faint plume of exhaust. Mason handed them to Rovski.

It really was all connected, he realized—all of it. He'd seen this before, in the stadium with Herman, anticipating a ball game. The tiny ball in that massive space was like this spacecraft in the void. It was an elegant parallel, or maybe it was the same thing seen from a different state of mind. Ned and Rovski were just as enthralled as he was, gaping at the spectacle, which was reassuring. It meant he wasn't crazy.

The whole dream thing felt like a lot of work, and it seemed raw, and sloppy, like he was acquiring new skills at a primitive level. Like when he'd dragged the bow across the violin's strings at Peggy's school. But musicians honed their skills through practice, until they sounded as polished as Asha did. Mason could definitely get a handle on this shifted consciousness thing. Not right away, but he'd get there. He was just getting started.

●●●●●●●

Also from Dagmar Miura

The Mason Braithwaite Paranormal Mystery Series

No one is ever quite sure whether psychic investigator Mason gets results with actual psychic power or his more mundane flatfooting, but the disheveled redhead manages to resolve some intractable mysteries.

mason.dagmarmiura.com

Penstock Canyon

While helping out a friend suffering from late-night visitations, psychic investigator Mason is confronted with aliens on the roof and other liminal beings that have him questioning the very nature of reality.

mason.dagmarmiura.com

The Slater Ibáñez Books

Don't mess with the hothead, or he might just mess with you. The first book in the series sees the insurance investigator running surveillance on an injured tech worker and tangling with blackmailers, party girls, late-night hookups with a gamut of guys, and a lot of bourbon.

slater.dagmarmiura.com

Brawl in Bardo

Slater spends the night in a dusty Mojave Desert town and finds that things look different in the space between LA and Vegas, like the bardo between lives. Soon he's stalking a sleazy dermatologist who's in a custody battle with another croaker for a seemingly worthless statue.

slater.dagmarmiura.com

Truman and Celeste

Sometimes all a woman needs is a decent man—even if she's not sleeping with him. Join Truman and Celeste as they troll the gritty underbelly of Los Angeles, never hesitating to slam that cocktail, hit on guys, or ask the next relevant question.

truman.dagmarmiura.com

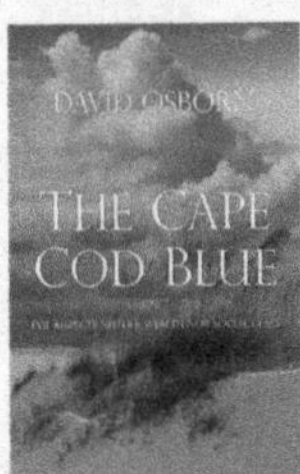

The Cape Cod Blue

The glittering, exalted world of art auctioning hides love, hate, and parricidal murder in a wealthy and socially prominent family when forgery of an anonymous Cape Cod painting is used to steal a world-famous portrait that's worth a fortune.

capecod.dagmarmiura.com

The Bone Bridge

Yarrott Benz, the 2016 Ippy Award winner for memoir, is forced to deal with extraordinary self-sacrifice in this harrowing account of teenage brothers, as different as night and day, trapped together in a dramatic medical dilemma.

bonebridge.dagmarmiura.com

The Psychic Vegan Cookbook

It has never been easier to cook vegan, and you don't even need to be psychic to do it. Whether your motivation is eating healthier or the welfare of other sentient creatures, Henrietta Flores guides you through plant-based versions of familiar dishes.

cookbook.dagmarmiura.com